LETTERS FROM
A SLAVE GIRL

LETTERS FROM A SLAVE GIRL

THE STORY OF
HARRIET JACOBS

MARY E. LYONS

CHARLES SCRIBNER'S SONS
NEW YORK
Maxwell Macmillan Canada
Toronto
Maxwell Macmillan International
New York   Oxford   Singapore   Sydney

Charles Scribner's Sons Books for Young Readers
Macmillan Publishing Company
866 Third Avenue; New York, NY 10022

Maxwell Macmillan Canada, Inc.
1200 Eglinton Avenue East, Suite 200
Don Mills, Ontario M3C 3N1

Macmillan Publishing Company is part of
the Maxwell Communication Group of Companies.

First edition   10 9 8 7 6 5 4 3 2 1
Printed in the United States of America

Library of Congress Cataloging-in-Publication Data
Lyons, Mary (Mary E.)
    Letters from a slave girl : the story of Harriet Jacobs / Mary E. Lyons.
—1st. ed.
        p.   cm.   Includes bibliographical references.
    Summary: A fictionalized version of the life of Harriet Jacobs, told in the form of letters that she might have written during her slavery in North Carolina and as she prepared for escape to the North in 1842.
    ISBN 0-684-19446-5
    1. Jacobs, Harriet A. (Harriet Ann), 1813–1897—Juvenile fiction.
[1. Jacobs, Harriet A. (Harriet Ann), 1813–1897—Fiction.   2. Slavery—Fiction.
3. Afro-Americans—Fiction.   4. Letters—Fiction.]   I. Title.
PZ7.L99556Le   1992   [Fic]—dc20   91-45778

*To all women everywhere
who seek to escape their oppression*

CONTENTS

ACKNOWLEDGMENTS

I am grateful to the Virginia Foundation for the Humanities and Public Policy for a fellowship to complete this book. Thanks also to the staffs of the North Carolina State Archives, the Museum of Early Southern Decorative Arts, and the Museum of the Albemarle. Special thanks to Art Collier for his literary insight and to Linda Bodlak-Brown for her helpful suggestions. I am also grateful to Kimberly Connor and Elizabeth Baer, two women's-studies scholars who, in the true spirit of Harriet Jacobs, shared their resources with me. Finally, thanks always to my husband, Paul Collinge, who still gives me love and books.

LETTERS FROM
A SLAVE GIRL

PART I
1825–1833

Mama

Dear Mama,

I write this letter to tell you Miss Margaret Horniblow dying. You know she is always been sickly, even when you were alive. This morning Docter Norcom come. He brung his black bag, and soon as he take out the lancet and bleeding cup I know the Missus bad off. I never did see a person get well after the Docter finish his bleeding cure.

Little while ago, Missus ask for me. A-laying up in that big old four-poster bed, she look like a pale white heron bird. Her eyes all glassy-like. Alone with her, I was afraid. Then Miss Margaret slip this old account Book into my hand. Harriet, she whisper, you read the Bible and practice your letters. Most Slave children dont get any learning, she say, now dont waste it. Then she turn her head away. The Docter, he come back and scat me out the door.

My little Book is fill with numbers and lists. If I turn it over and upside down, I can write on the back side of each page. The blue leather all faded. Feel soft, like John's bottom when he was just a little baby thing.

3

Mama, I am not so lonesome if I can talk to you in my Book.

Your daughter,
Harriet Ann

* * *

3 July, 1825

Dear Mama,

This letter is letting you know Miss Margaret Horniblow die at dawn. Docter Norcom brung his wife, Maria, and she put silver dollers on the Missus' eyes to keep them close. That is only right, since she Miss Margaret's sister.

Well, my own eyes is red and puffy today. Miss Margaret been almost a mother to me since you left this world five long years ago. I love her like I love you. It might hurt you to hear that, but I cant help it. Missus, she keep her promise. Do you remember how she hold your hand when you were so sick? Gran has tell me the story every time I ask her. Dont fret, Delilah, Missus say to you the night you die. I'll take care of your Harriet. And Mama, she did.

Miss Margaret show me how to sew teensy stitches and knots and how to use the silver thimble you give me. And she teach me to read and spell. I am teaching my own self how to write.

Your Harriet Ann

* * *

4

Dear Mama,

Missus buried today in the little churchyard. Daddy walk with me to the cemetery. We wait behind the hemlock tree till the White folks gone, then stand by her grave. When my tears fall on the fresh durt, Daddy wrap his big rough hand round mine, but he dont cry at all. His face look as hard as the headstones that stand watch over that quiet place.

He dont say, but I know what the trouble is.

Ever since Mister Knox die and leave Daddy to his daughter, he been living and working on his own. The old man say in his will that Daddy is an old and faithful servant and can buy his freedom for 300 doller.

So he been traveling round like a free man long as I can remember. His missus let him stay at his workshop. In return he pay her two hundred a year, a little each month. And all this time he been putting money aside to buy him self.

But lass year young missus marry the master of Green Hall. Now the new master thinking he might hire Daddy out and keep the earnings for him self. And Daddy feeling mad bout it. Seem like he is always hot as red peppers bout something anyway. Yelling at me and Little John and fussing at us for no good reason.

But for all that, Mama, you would be proud as ever of him. He still a fine carpenter, and folks round here always asking for Daniel Jacobs to do a job of work. And he have a choice new set of tools. Ax, chisel, saw, and some I dont know the name of or what they do.

Mama, do you think Miss Margaret going to set me free

in her will? I ask Daddy on the way back to town, but his back got stiff as Gran's broom. In the eyes of God you already free, he say. Then he look strate ahead and clamp his lips down tight all the way to King Street.

Your daughter,
Harriet Ann

*   *   *

7 July, 1825

Dear Mama,

I been staying with Gran at Horniblow's Tavern till Miss Margaret's will read next week. Lass year her mother, Miss Elizabeth, move to her farm out on Horniblow Point. She be renting the tavern to Mr. O'Malley, and Gran go along with it for an extra 20 dollers. Now old Missus got a little more money floating in her pocket becaus she own a good cook.

Daddy went to Green Hall, so John staying here instead of the workshop. Can you see your Son from where you are, Mama? He is small for a 9-year-old, and quick as a deer. But he dont have much sense, if you ask me.

Like this morning. When Gran turn her back to pull the bread loaves out of the oven, John say, Hatty! Race you down to the water! We slip out the back door and he take off like a hunting dog, hollering Pokey! at me over his shoulder. He win that race in less than a minute, but guess why? Only becaus he cut through White folks' yards to do it. John S Jacobs is just like Daddy. He still dont think he is a Slave.

We sat on the loading dock at the warehouse and watch a schooner come in from Charleston. John's jaw drop when he see all those muscley-looking men roll hundreds of

6

barrels of rum down to the wharf. Then they turn right round and throw huge bales of cotton up on the ship's deck. It been early morning, not even the heat of the day, but sweat drip off their backs like rain off a roof.

Listen, Mama. I did something mean. John looking at big trouble soon if somebody dont wake him up to the facts. I say, John S Jacobs, you might have to sweat your life out on those wharves for a master one day.

I dont know I been a Slave till I was six, say I. Never even heared the word till after Mama die. But I learn quick enough. Now it is time you quit acting free. Or you be toss like a sack of turnips in that new white brick jail they just build behind the courthouse. And they be clanging the iron door shut!

John look at me like he dont even hear what I am saying. He just laugh and remind me I am suppose to weed Gran's patch before lunch. Then he dare me to race him back to the tavern through Mr Josiah Collins's yard. I holler No! and tell him it is not safe to fool round the house of the richest man in these parts, especially since he own our Uncle Joseph.

Anyway, Mama, Gran say I am growing into a Woman soon. And I guess Women dont run races with little boys, do they? Leastways, I have not seen such.

Your Harriet Ann

*　*　*

8 July, 1825

Dear Mama,

I like being at the tavern with Gran. It is noisy, but I eat anytime I want. And I can see clear down to the bay when I look out the side window. Gran up after midnight making

7

pound cakes to sell this morning. When I wake up the kitchen smell all sweet and sugary. Then I hear her laughing with Mrs Wills's Woman, Rachel. Going on bout how many pastries Mrs W can eat at one time. They quit giggling when a White Woman come jingling coins, calling for Yeller Molly to count out three dozen of her good crackers.

I been learning how to make crackers. First I sift flour till Gran say I look dusty as a miller. Then she dump everything in a big bowl and show me how to cut in the butter and stir in the milk. Hard part was rolling out the dough. It stuck like pine tar to the rolling pin and the table and even my face.

Gran keeps the receipt in her head but I have to write it out to remember: 1 pound flour, 1 pony glass of sugar, 4 good pinches of salt, butter the size of an egg, and ½ glass milk. Roll, cut, prick with a fork, and bake in a hot oven till light golden. Like the color of my skin, Gran say.

Do you know she still hide her baking money? Since you left, nobody know where it is except Daddy. I think he give Gran all his savings when he leave for Green Hall. He growl something bout not being able to trust plantation folk. But they probably say the same bout us town coloureds.

Mama, Gran still has that old dream bout buying her children. Even with you gone, there is still three left to save for: Aunt Betty and Uncle Mark and Uncle Joseph. And me and John. Well, except for Uncle Joseph, who belong to Mister Collins, Miss Margaret own us all. Even Aunt Betty, except she been loaned out to the Norcoms since they got married. Who going to own us now? Not Gran, I think, if crackers only cost a few coppers.

8

And this will break your heart. Miss Elizabeth Horniblow let Gran keep her baking money, but guess who
come nocking at Gran's door, asking could she borrow
three hundred doller? Imagine, Gran say after she leave,
my Missus borrowing money from her own Slave!

I been making my prayers as strong as I can and reading
the Bible. Things might brighten up. Today Gran plop a
bowl of corn bread and molasses on the table, then sit
right down and look at me hard while I eat. Girl, she say,
you got a shine on your face. What you so happy bout?

Mama, tell me this. Gran know what I think almost
before I do. How come it? Becaus I feel sort of shivery
inside. Like good news on its way!

Your sweet girl,
Harriet

*   *   *

9 July, 1825

Dear Mama,

Tomorrow be the most important day of my eleven years.
The lawyers, they reading Miss Margaret's will at the
courthouse. I know I been her favorite, and all my friends
think she has leave me free. Freedom! The word taste like
Christmas when I say it out loud. Like a juicy orange or
a cup of sweetened milk.

Gran is always been a hopeful person, like you, Mama.
But she say she cant let Hope in the door. You all worth
too much money, Gran tell me. She recall that Mark worth
100 doller when he was only a boy of twelve, and now he
a grown man of twenty-five. Slaves over eighteen but
under thirty bring the high bid, she say. And we dont

even speak of the Slave-trader. Like death. If we dont talk bout it, maybe it wont happen.

But I am not afraid to hope. Not when I remember Miss Margaret Horniblow and you grow up like sisters. Gran, she say she nurse you both. You were like twins, least till Miss Elizabeth made Gran wean you at three months to make sure Margaret getting enough milk. And Gran tell me you and Miss Margaret play together when you too young to understand the White girl be owning the Black one.

I know Miss Margaret has remember her childhood friend and the promise she make the night you die. Besides, she her self taught me to read these words from the Bible: Thou shalt love thy neighbor as thyself.

Tomorrow I taste freedom.

Your loving daughter,
Harriet Ann

* * *

10 July, 1825

Dear Mama,

A long, sad day. Gran fix breakfast, make five chicken pies, and walk back and forth from the tavern to the court-house to Docter Norcom's house. She hoping to hear news of the will from Aunt Betty. Aunt Betty say a good house-keeper shut her mouth and open her ears. That way she know everything going on inside *and* outside the White folks' house.

John and I, we get tired of stoking Gran's bake oven, so we sneak down to the water. We play tag round the cannons in front of Mister Collins house and watch the buoys out in the bay. John, he say the buoys remind him of old Josiah Collins's him self because they bob up and down like a duck. Then he act a fool and walk like a duck. But I been too anxious to laugh, so I shove him to make him stop.

After sunset we run back to the tavern. My heart flop when I see Gran coming up the path through the shadows. From the look on her face, I know she feeling raggedy.

She do not speak a word, but sink to her cane-bottom chair and make a hunh sound, like somebody nock the breath out of her with a stick. Lord, child, she finally say. Margaret Horniblow has give you to her niece. Your new missus is a child of three! You going to live with Docter Norcom and his wife Maria and their children. But you be special maid to their little Mary Matilda.

Gran look tired and worn-out as that old homespun quilt I sleep under. And what bout John, and Aunt Betty, and Uncle Mark? I ask. Well, Gran sigh, she give them back to her mother.

Seem like our family been passed round like a jug of ten-cent whiskey at the tavern table. First we all belong to the old missus, Elizabeth Horniblow. Then we been given to her daughter, Margaret. Now all the property of Miss Elizabeth again except me, and I go to Margaret's niece! And nobody going free.

I dont like this Docter Norcom so very much. He might sell me. Auction me like some farm plow to a plantation up the Chowan River. To think of it give me a deep sick feeling. You know a plantation master, he usually wait till a Slave child is twelve before putting her on a hoe gang in the cotton. But my birthday coming soon!

11

And every year I hear bout field hands falling right out in the killing summer heat. Mama, I cant write anymore.

Harriet Ann

*   *   *

September, 1825

Dear Mama,

Have you been missing my letters? The Norcoms, they keeping me too busy. It is a strange household. Docter Norcom and Missus Maria, they is cold folk. They dont hardly speak a kind word, even to each other. Docter Norcom, he forever preaching little sermons to his children. He act like he a docter of the church instead of a docter of medicine.

Aunt Betty say Missus leave home too young. She only sixteen when she marry the Docter, and he almost old enough to be her Daddy! She been having babies ever since, and it has wore her down. Aunt Betty tell me living with a rip-jack old man has made Missus Maria stingy too.

I guess that is how come we dont get enough to eat. Sometimes only the leftover gravy, with no biscuit. Missus dont like us going over to see Gran, but I make sure every errand take me by the tavern. Gran always got a thick slice of wheat bread with preserves for me to share with little John.

Mama, you'd a-been crying along with me when Elizabeth Horniblow turn John over to Docter Norcom to be his shop boy. You know the weight of Slavery always been heavy on Daddy's shoulders, and he is pass this on to his Son. John fights back, but in this house he going to pay for it.

12

First thing the Docter do is forbid his Sons to teach John how to read and write. I know Daddy always want us to get book learning, but there will be no ABC for John. Well, the Docter, he cant take away what I already got, except I be writing letters in secret now. And knowing John, he be teaching his own self how to read and write.

Harriet Ann

*   *   *

October, 1825

Dear Mama,

I wish you were here, cause John is bout to worry me to death. Lass week he was playing ball with some White boys on the courthouse green. Somebody, and John wont tell who, broke two courthouse window.

Now there's a sign posted saying: Every person convicted of breaking the courthouse windows by playing ball against the building pays a fine of 5 doller for each pane of glass so broken. Sound strict, dont it?

But listen to this, Mama! Every Slave committing the same offence will be punished by whipping not exceeding thirty-nine lashes. And who is out there playing ball again today? You exactly right. I dont think Gran could stand it if John was tore up by the lash. Daddy be mad, or I'd get him to talk to John.

We see Daddy every now and again at the tavern. He still traveling round to different jobs, but he cant keep any money for him self. It hurt him to see John and me living in the Norcom house. He want to buy our freedom with his savings, but they wont do business with a Slave.

I guess that is why his temper hot as July. He yell at

us to hate Slavery. I try to remember he holler becaus he love us.

Always a hundred chores to do. I sew endless plain seam for the Norcom boys' pantaloons and help Aunt Betty with cooking and cleaning. Yesterday we soak cucumber in brine till my fingers shrivel up from the saltwater.

Today we clean the parlor. The Docter come in when I was dusting those little round paintings hanging on the wall. He say be careful with his miniatures, especially the one of the Great Docter Benjamin Rush. This Rush must be something special, becaus one of the Norcom boy is name after him. The Docter bragging that Rush taught him heroic medicine. But Rush dont look like a hero to me. Just another old White man in a fancy coat.

All my other time spent with Mary Matilda. I do get tired of watching her for hours at a stretch. Still, she sweet, and her baby talk make me smile. Today I make her a doll from dress muslin. Young missus sit on my lap and we pat out the Juber song with the doll's arms: Juber up and juber down, juber all round the town. With Aunt Betty's company, a little song singing, and Gran's bread, I get through each day.

Your H

Daddy

24 December, 1826

Dear Daddy,

Christmas Week dont seem the same with out you to bring
us wooden pull-toys and a wild duck for Christmas supper.
When you went away lass spring, me and John was left to
the mursey of this wurld. John say Slavery made you
sicken and die. When you couldn't save money for freedom, he say, you felt like a possum trapped in a tree. He
is not over it yet.

Lass night I tell him, John, a brighter day coming! He
say, you dont know anything bout it, Hatty! We never
going to be free! Hurt my feelings when he raise his voice,
even though he dont mean it.

Today we visit Providence burying ground. The plain
wooden board with your name on it look respectable,
except I am the only one who can read the words. The
little tree you plant on Mama's grave seven years ago is
now taller than John. Gran and I brush away the leaves
that had fall on you and Mama.

That sorrowful job make me remember the day you die,

and how the Missus wont let me go see you laid out in your pine coffin. Instead I gather flowers to pretty up her house for a tea. Mrs Maria Norcom is the perfect picture of meanness.

Does having babies make a Woman mean? Becaus Missus had another girl baby a month before you die, and she might be expecting again.

I miss you, Daddy, even though I am mad with you for leaving us. I guess that make me your daughter, since you always were mad as hops bout every little thing. I hope you happier now.

Your girl,
Harriet

* * *

25 December, 1826

Dear Daddy,

John feeling better some today. He all smiley becaus we got a week's rest from chores. Some days we work from dawn to way past dark. Gran call it working from can to cant.

We been up early this morning, but not to work. The hole house got up to see the Johnkannaus coming down Broad. They beating the gumbo box, playing triangles and jawbones, and singing made-up songs. And dancing through the street like turkeys walking through molasses. Lawsy, Aunt Betty say, what a sight!

Daddy, do you remember the Christmas Day when John run into the crowd and get lost? Gran have a fit becaus her grandbaby mix up with those common plantation Slaves dressed in cow tails and horns. You know Gran dont approve of dancing, much less begging at White folks' door for a penny or glass of rum.

Even the Norcoms crack their faces to laugh when the coloureds come to the door. And they dont dare hold back the coppers, or the beggars be singing loud enough for all the neighbors to hear:

> Poor massa, so they say,
> Down in the heel, so they say,
> Got no money, so they say,
> Not one shilling, so they say,
> God A'mighty bless you, so they say.

Everybody in Edenton know Docter Norcom, becaus he see so many sick folk. And he worry bout what the town think of him. Lass thing he want is people saying he got no money.

The Norcoms give me and John each an orange. I sew John a shirt from scraps becaus he hate those rough white shirts made of negro cloth. Gran give me some old account Books she save from the tavern. They is bigger than Miss Margaret's blue Book and even got a few blank pages. I will write more letters to you, Daddy. I am getting over my mad spell. Merry Christmas from your

Harriet

*   *   *

26 January, 1827

Dear Daddy,

I write you with gloves on. It is so cold the Albemarle Sound is froze clear across to Tyrell County. They say it is been the coldest winter since 1781, when the Sound was twelve mile of solid ice.

The temperature got down to thirteen degrees lass Friday and Saturday, and even Gran dont go to church on Sunday. I sneak a look at Docter Norcom's Edenton Gazette, which report in fancy words that a party of gentlemen had dinner out on the ice lass Monday. Some folk got more time than sense.

Aunt Betty and I come inside to sleep by the fireplace till the weather break. The Norcoms let me sleep with her in the outbuilding unless Mary Matilda is sick and need nursing. They still let Betty keep her little room out there—the one they give her after she marry Stephen the Sailor and keep losing her unborn babies, one by one.

I ask Aunt Betty to tell me bout having babies, but she dont talk about it except to Gran. I ask Gran bout having babies, but she say, Hush, child, you too young. My friend Chloe, who belong to Mrs Gardner, jump the broom with Moss McDonald at Christmas, and now she expecting a baby in March. I ask her how come the baby get here so quick, but she dont know. I wish I could ask Mama.

Too cold to write more.

Your H

* * *

February, 1827

Dear Daddy,

You would raise revolution if you saw what happen yesterday. I been punish by the Missus for the first time. Gran, she take my old negro shoes—even with the extra pieces of leather sewed on, I had wore holes in the side.

So she buy me a new pair at the market house, but the thick wood soles creak when I walk.

Missus say, What makes that horrid noise? I show her my shoes. Take them off, she order me, and if you put them on again, I'll throw them into the fire.

It was snowing out, but I say, Yes, Ma'am. Then she send me on an errand, and my feet burn when I dash through the snow. I go to bed lass night with a sore throat, and I know sure as the world that I will die in the night. But I wake up to the bad news that I am still alive and still a Slave.

I sneak over to Gran today. She nod and listen and give me as much sponge cake as I want. Her smile dry my tears and the big fireplace warm my feet. But Daddy, nothing going to melt that lump of ice called Mrs Maria Norcom.

Your daughter,
Harriet Ann

*   *   *

17 March, 1827

Dear Daddy,

Chloe had her baby this morning. Aunt Betty say she had a hard time, but I dont know why. Says she will tell me later.

And tell Mama I read in the paper that Mrs Catharine Gardner's other Woman, Lucy, run away January lass. When Gran brung over some corn bread this morning, she tell me that Mama and Lucy been friends growing up. She guess becaus they both so light-skin.

Aunt Betty say Lucy's husband run away from his master

lass summer, and Lucy is likely gone to meet him somewhere in the Northern States. There is a 5 doller reward for Lucy and 20 for her man. I hope they is free and safe, becaus their story is a sweet one to me.

Then Gran and Aunt Betty, they chatter on bout how Lucy's husband is six feet tall and well made. I cant hear the rest becaus they start talking low. I give out the hint that it is awful rude to be whispering, but they say they tell me later. I hope these later stories worth the wait.

John is lately acting like a fool. Lass Tuesday a schooner call Harriet sail in. It was a big ship, loaded with groceries, hardware, and tools. John tease me no end, Daddy. Say if I dont quit eating so much pound cake, I be growing big as a boat.

That is not likely in the Norcom household.

Your Harriet Ann

* * *

17 April, 1827

Dear Daddy,

Mrs Catharine Gardner must be a mighty hard Missus. Chloe has ran away, too. There is a 10 doller reward if she is deliver to the Slave-ketcher or turn over to the constable at the jail.

Do you remember Mrs Gardner's housekeeper, Aggy? She been close friend with Gran for years. Chloe run away with Aggy's daughter,, and they both show up at Gran's door, begging her to keep Chloe's infant child. But Gran say she too old to be raising any more children.

I found her crying today. Say she let her friend down.

I try to comfort her, but that is hard for me becaus Gran dont yet know what is happen to John.

Yesterday he come home with scratches on his face. Been fighting with the young master, James Norcom, Jr. I yell at him, John! A twelve-year-old Slave with good sense dont fight his seventeen-year-old master! John says, Hatty, he try to tie my hands behind my back and whip me for no reason. You taught John to hate Slavery, Daddy, but not how to hide the hate.

And the Docter getting meaner every day. This morning I was on my hands and knees scrubbing the hall floor. He come in and start looking at me hard, like a bird watching for a worm. Then he try to talk, if you want to call it that. But talk take two, and I wouldn't turn my head to him. Just keep pushing that scrub brush round and round, while he remind me I am made for his use. You must obey my command in *every* thing, he say.

Daddy, I do all they say. What more do he want?

Harriet Ann

*   *   *

27 December, 1827

Dear Daddy,

Christmas Week, rest, and finally time for my Book. Mary Matilda been sick with the croup—I been sleeping on the floor next to her trundle bed, bringing tea and hot toweling to loosen her chest.

She is up and bout now, so I can make new britches for John and a real woollen dress for myself. That shapeless sack Missus Norcom give me every winter make me look like a potato! And the linsey-woolsey is rough on my skin.

Besides, it mark me as a Slave. Wish I could wear bough-ten clothes like the free coloureds in Edenton buy from Northern ships. But there is a lot to wish for round here.

Gran is tolerably well. And Aunt Betty been smiling like a cat becaus Uncle Stephen come home from sea on Christmas Day. Been sashaying in from her little house every morning, acting all secrety. Gran say it was a good thing Mary Matilda had the croup and I had to sleep inside the big house.

Yours,
Harriet

*   *   *

28 December, 1827

Dear Daddy,

The weather turn cold lass night and Gran's Missus took ill. Gran say she might be in her lass sickness. She been nursing her till I worry bout Gran getting sick, too. With this cold snap seem like John had to split and tote firewood all the long day. It is Christmas Week, but there is some chores we never free of.

He grumble bout it, but he is helping me make new mattress ticks. I stitch the homespun cloth into sacks, and he stuff them with fresh wheat straw. Lass summer I lay by some dirty cotton left on the wharf. John going to mix it with straw and change the stuffing in the pillow ticks. It cheer me up to have fresh bedding, even if it is not a chicken-feather mattress like Gran got.

Your daughter,
Harriet Ann Jacobs

*   *   *

29 December, 1827

Dear Daddy,

Old Missus, Elizabeth Horniblow, die today. Gran say her time had come. They has laid her out in winding sheets on the cooling board, and she be buried tomorrow. The Docter, he in charge of her estate, I guess becaus he married to her daughter, and the only man left in the family.

I been letting myself dream that Missus leave Gran free. Miss Elizabeth promise Gran that freedom be at the end of all these years of service. But Daddy, you and I both know *that* promise can be empty as a Slave's pocket. Gran, she dont say it out loud, but I read her feelings as easy as I read the Bible. Her eyes tell me she is letting Hope slip its foot in the door.

Your daughter,
Harriet Ann

*   *   *

30 December, 1827

Dear Daddy,

The Horniblow and Norcom Slaves went to Miss Elizabeth's funeral. Preacher tell the family what a fine Christian Miss Elizabeth been. After the service, Gran ask the Docter bout the 300 doller Elizabeth Horniblow borrow and promise to pay back.

Oh, no, Aunt Molly, I heared him say, the estate is insolvent and the law prohibits payment. Gran dont understand all the words, but she understand what they mean: There will be no 300 doller. Miss Elizabeth use the money to buy a silver candelabra. I guess Maria Norcom going to inherit it and I be polishing it soon. The will is read tomorrow.

Harriet Ann

*   *   *

31 December, 1827

Dear Daddy,

Miss Elizabeth keep her word. She leave Gran a free woman. But the wishes of the dead dont mean nothing to a man with honor as flimsy as a dead cornstalk! The Docter, he say Gran must be sold. And Mark and John, too! Aunt Betty, she stay on with the Norcoms.

From what Aunt Betty heared round the house, Norcom mean to buy John from the estate so he can own him outright. But if a Slave-trader buy Gran or Mark, they might be gone from here forever. Feel like I'm drowning—half my family going to the auction block on Hiring Day.

Docter and the Missus already own a fine house, a big farm, seven lots, and nineteen Slaves. But Aunt Betty say they land-rich and cash-poor. Norcom's greed is dark and foul, like the water sitting at the end of Queen Anne's Creek. I do despise him, but Gran say it is all God's will. Well, I know what you would say.

Your Harriet

*   *   *

Dear Daddy,

I am glad it was God's will to make Gran a clever woman, becaus she is outfox the Docter. John and I meet Gran and Mark early this morning at the Market House. I dont read the posted sign to them, but they know what it mean: PUBLIC SALE OF NEGROES AND HORSES.

Gangs of Slaves were milling round like prisaners waiting for the sentence. I did not let myself look at the faces of the Women with children for sale. My heart too full of misery to feel anything else.

Gran act meek, as usual, but she have a secret smile that worry me. Say Norcom want to get rid of her at a private sale, to save her pride, he claim, but she refuse. Harriet, Gran tell me, I want the wurld to see his shame! If he selling me, then let him do it in public. Let everybody see he is a thief who have stole my freedom! Gran's high spirit dont make me feel a bit better, so I hold her hand all morning. I link our fingers together like a chain strong as the one they put on Slaves in jail.

Well, first come the Hiring Out. The Slaves crowd round the good masters, the ones they know give out a blanket at Christmas and biscuit every Sunday. Please, massa, hire me this year, they beg. I will work *very* hard, massa.

Then Slaves for sale brung up. Everybody recognize Gran when she climb on the block. They been eating her cake and crackers for years. They also know Miss Elizabeth meant for her to go free.

Oh, Daddy, I love the look on old Norcom's face when the White folks call out, Shame! Shame! Who is going to sell *you*, Aunt Molly? Dont stand there! That's no place for you!

The sheriff, he hold up Gran's arm and announce to the crowd, I have Yellow Molly Horniblow here! Who will start the bidding for this fine cook?

I hold my breath, waiting to hear what my dear Gran is worth in cold cash. She stand still as a stone. Not one soul bid.

Suddenly, a soft voice call out, fifty. The voice belong to Hannah, Miss Elizabeth's sister. She been knowing Gran for forty years. Had tea with her just lass week. Nobody raise the bid, and I let out my breath. Guess the other White folk got too much respect for Gran's high reputation and Miss Hannah's seventy years.

Then they put Mark on the block. Every time the price go up, Miss Hannah speak out in her faint voice and go a little higher. Finally she pay 400 doller for my Uncle Mark. Then it was John's turn. Just like Aunt Betty thought. When the hammer come down, he been sold to Norcom for 298 doller and 50 cent.

Hannah dont read or write, and sign the bill of sale with an X. I say a prayer of thanks when her palsy hand make that shaky mark. We were lucky. A very old man went for 1 doller and an old cook for 17. Another Woman been offer for 20 doller to anyone willing to take her away. These poor souls be treated like work horses, all broke down.

John is bitter now that he under Norcom's compleat control. I try to comfort him. We all still together, I remind him, and Gran is safe. At least as safe as a Slave can be.

Your daughter,
Harriet Ann

Mama

Dear Mama,

My first dance come bout becaus of you.

Well, the master at Hayes plantation tell his people they can have a sociable this Saturday night. Weather been warm all winter, and folk saying the persimmon beer they make lass fall is bout right. And Uncle Mark, he say any master let the Slaves have some fun is a smart man.

You being Gran's daughter, I guess you know what she think bout it. She set her jaw and say, No, Harriet, you cant go. Then a tear big as the end of my finger slip down my face. Dont be crying to me, she say, becaus Miss Maria wont let you run round at night, anyhow.

Then I remember, Mama! You told me once that you and Daddy met at a dance. So I say real nice: Gran, if it weren't for dancing, Mama and Daddy wouldn't never have got together. And if it weren't for them getting together, you wouldn't have me and John to love you. And if you didn't have me and John to love you . . . Then Gran got all crabbed and cut me off.

But first thing you know, she has spoke to the Missus.

27

And Cousin Fanny is telling me she going to walk with me over to Hayes. Fanny, she been staying with Gran ever since Gran moved into a little cottage on King Street. And I guess it is God's will that she is round to take me to the dance. This be one time when God and I see eyeball to eyeball bout His will.

Yours ever,
Harriet Ann

*   *   *

Sunday Night

Dear Mama,

I found the best beau! He is a long tall young man, the color of warm brown velvet. Out of all the girls at the frolic, he notice me! Everybody wear their finest. There were grapevine hoops on some of the petticoats. And one girl had store her dress in herbs and dried flowers, so she smell sweet every time she float by.

I stitch up a buff calico dress with pearl buttons, and John make me a necklace of dried chinaberries. And paint it red to match the red ribbon I wind in my braids. But my young man say it was my sweet face he saw first.

There was a fine big band. Two fiddle, gourd banjo, wood flute, triangle, and bones. First we kick our shoes off to dance. Those hard old shoes make too much noise and hurt the feet.

Then the fiddlers play the boys' favorite tune: Going to the East, Going to the West. They like it becaus one of the steps call for a kiss. But dont get upset, Mama. It was respectable. We stand a foot apart with out touching hands, only lips. Seem like that dance been the happiest three minute of my fourteen years!

28

When folk got tired of dancing, there was beer and roasted sweet potato. But we never did wear it out. Just dance till Fanny say, Harriet, time to go. There was a big mush-melon moon, and my fellow, he want to walk me home. But I know Gran would say that was *fast* courting.

Besides, I be seeing him round. He live in the neighborhood. Like Daddy, he is a carpenter and a good one. Except he is a free-born man!

Your happy girl,
Harriet

* * *

March, 1828

Dear Mama,

Day has turn to night. The Docter, he been whispering filthy words in my ear. I know what he want, and I am shamed for him and me both.

He follow me everywhere. It's got so I look over my shoulder all the time. Today I step out on the piazza for a bit of air. Soon I heared footsteps and a low voice reminding me, You are my property.

Lass week I walk over to Providence to lay a bouquet of Snow Drops on your grave. A shadow fall over me when I kneel down. Then I turn and see the Docter, and it scare me so bad I almost run. I wont touch you, he say, but dont forget who you belong to. Then he say, One day you must yeild to me.

I long to tell Gran, but you know how strict she is bout Womanish things. If it weren't for listening to other Women at quiltings and such, I wouldnt know anything bout making babies. Now I know what makes a baby, but I'm still not too sure how they get here.

And even if I let out what Norcom wants, Gran might get her self in trouble. Aunt Betty has tell me a story bout your sister, Becky. Say when Beck was near my age, a White gentleman insult her. Gran was so put out that she run after him with a loaded pistol. Aunt Beck dead and gone, but Gran might still have that pistol!

Your H

* * *

April, 1828

Dear Mama,

Thinking bout R help me forget my trouble with the Docter. (I dont dare write his name, Mama, in case Norcom find my Book!) I seen him at a few more dances and sometimes on the street.

And he fill up my thoughts, dont matter what the chore. Darning socks, sowing seed, walking Mary Matilda to school—R's face swim in front of me, like my own when I look in the rain bucket.

The Docter, he know there is somebody special, but not who it is. He dont lay a hand on me, but he think of little ways to bend my will to his. Lass week he ketch me writting to Fanny. Now he slip notes into my hand. When I claim I cant read them, he read them to me and say, Do you understand? I understand too much, Mama. What do I do?

Your Harriet

* * *

10 April, 1828

Dear Mama,

I write with good news. A tiny X has change our lives again. Gran be a free woman! Miss Hannah ask the Judge could he emancipate Gran, and the papers is all signed.

Then Miss Hannah, she let Gran buy Uncle Mark. Except Gran had to use him as security before they make her free. So he can be sold at any time to pay her debts.

If only you and Daddy could have been with us all tonight, sitting by the fire. Gran and Mark keep grinning at each other and passing the papers back and forth. And asking me to read them out loud, till I think the words be in my head forever: That whereas Negro woman Molly lately the property of the above Hannah Pritchard hath this day been emancipated and freed by the Superior Court of Law of Chowan County, North Carolina.

Uncle Mark tell Gran how proud he is of her, and she tell him, we been taking care of others for so long. Now we going to prove to the wurld we can take care of our own selves.

Then I make sure Gran remember the law. You cant travel anywhere with out a pass, I warn her, or the pat-tyrollers whip you if they ketch you. They put you in jail, and if you cant pay the fine, you back at the beginning. One slip and you a Slave again.

Gran is so wild with joy she dont half hear me. But she is got to know: Even with a pass, she can only travel one county beyond Chowan. And never to Virginia, since free coloureds cant enter that state.

31

Knowing Gran, she wont leave her family. But after fifty year of Slavery, there is nothing worth the risk of losing freedom.

Your daughter,
Harriet Ann

*   *   *

May, 1828

Dear Mama,

Docter Norcom, he do not let up. Been hard to keep on a-smiling for Gran and her good fortune when I be scared inside. Even harder to hide my feelings from Aunt Betty.

Lass night she say, Harriet, you use to have a light heart. When did it get so heavy and sad? Guess I just been growing up, I tell her. Norcom swear he will kill me if I talk, so I dont tell her or anyone, Mama. Only you.

Gran protect me with out knowing it. Norcom is afraid of her becaus everybody love her. He being a docter, he got to keep his reputation clean. He cant afford a public scorching by her tongue if she ketch him fooling with me.

And I am lucky to live in town. A plantation master have his way with any Slave he want, and nobody know the difference till a light-brown baby is born.

Your growing-up daughter,
Harriet Ann

*   *   *

September, 1828

Dear Mama,

Today Aunt Betty and I make pear preserves in the great iron kettle out behind the kitchen house. John, he lift the pot, but I tend the fire all day. I show Mary Matilda how to take up the fruit with a ladle. She think she is helping, but she ask a string of questions a mile long, then forget the answers. She dont seem to ketch on too quick. Missus, she stare at us from the back porch, quiet as a snake.

All summer long, Missus watch the Docter and the Docter watch me. He try one thing and then another. I would laugh if I were not so afraid. When he run out of words he make signs. I act like I dont understand, and then he cuss me for being stupid.

Have not seen R for weeks. He is working a job in Washington County. I cant eat much—the air been too hot and still. Feel like somebody threw a conjer spell over the hole town.

Harriet A

* * *

My Birthday, 1828

Dear Mama,

Weather finally broke. The air was clear and cool for my fifteen birthday. Gran bake a ginger cake in her Dutch oven and brung it over early. John swear he help make it. Claim he broke the sugar off the cone and beat the eggs. But Gran say, Harriet, your bragging brother did not do a lick except fetch chips and bark for the oven.

33

We had a little party out in the kitchen. John make fun of the preacher at St. Paul's. Say he look like the Dutch oven: squat with stumpy legs. Gran, she try not to laugh. She say, Boy, you worldly, too worldly. But John hard to ignore if he in a good mood. When he is not acting like Daddy, he give us a fine time.

Gran watch me close all morning. She know my spirit been down. Lass week she even try to buy me from Norcom, but he is too shrewd to let me go. Harriet does not belong to me, he answer her. She is my daughter's property, and I have no legal right to sell her.

This is a lie. He can do whatever he want with his Slaves. And what he want is to break my will. What he dont know is I am my

Father's daughter,
Harriet

*   *   *

September, 1828

Dear Mama,

R come back with a pocktful of money! He want to buy my freedom so I can marry him. He put his arm round my waist and say, Harriet, I know you dont love me, but will you have me? I laugh and say, Go along, R! If I dont love you, there's no water in the Chowan River!

At first I was too happy in myself to worry. But now I feel like two girl at once. One minute I'm smiling becaus I love my sweet R. Next I'm shaking becaus the Docter wont let it happen.

The Missus, she would love to see me sold. But what good it do her if I marry a local man and still be in her

34

sight? Besides, she think a Slave got no right to her own life.

Once I heared a Slave girl tell the Missus a young man want to marry her. Missus say, I will have you peeled and pickled if you mention the subject again. Mama, I would not look forward to being whipped and washed in brine.

Gran tell me getting marry is a serious business that lass a powerful long time. She say I am too young to marry R. But she want to bring a smile back to my face. I think she suspicion what Norcom been up to.

There is a White Woman in the neighborhood who is always been good to me. Gran say, Ask her to talk to the Docter and beg your case. So the lady say yes, she will speak to him tomorrow. Maybe my love-dream not over.

Your anxious
Harriet

*   *   *

Evening

Dear Mama,

Aunt Betty brung a message this morning: Docter wanting to see you in his study. The door was open. I walk in and stare at this man who thinks he some king can rule my body and heart.

So you want to be married, he say, and to a free nigger.

Yes, sir, I say softly. I swallow hard so I wont holler.

Well, if you *must* have a husband, you can take up with one of my Slaves, he say, acting all puffed-up and clever.

But when I turn this charity down, the Docter blow up

like a Thunderstorm. Never let me hear of that fellow again, he roar. If you even speak to him I will cowhide you and shoot him as soon as I would a dog.

Hate come over me strong today. I dont want to hear the preacher talk anymore bout hell, becaus I already been there.

Harriet

*   *   *

Late September, 1828

Dear Mama,

My dream is done. I turn this thing over in my mind till it come back on itself. Even if I could marry R, it would rain misery down on him to see me misused. Worse than that, our children be Slaves. Law say if the mama a Slave, then the baby is too.

So when R say he going to Savannah to look at some land, I say, Dont come back. Fly to the Free States, I cry, and make a life for Yourself! We weep on each other's necks, and he promise to return and buy me one day. I let him think it. But the Docter is a block of granite too hard and heavy to be moved.

Harriet Ann

*   *   *

20 October, 1828

Dear Mama,

Seem sad as a funeral round here. The leaves fading and falling, everything dying. The Docter has decide that Mary Matilda should sleep in his room. Being her maid,

I got to sleep on the floor in case she need me. I been safe in Aunt Betty's little house, but now there's no escape.

Harriet

* * *

21 October, 1828

Dear Mama,

The Missus find out what the Docter plan to do. She call me to her room this morning. First thing out of her mouth is, Did you know you were to sleep in the Docter's room?

Yes, ma'am, I say.

Who told you?

The master, I reply.

Will you answer truly all the questions I ask?

Yes, ma'am, I say, but I feel like I am sinking. I know the Missus dont want to hear the truth bout her husband. When she heared it, what would she do to me?

Then I had to sit on a stool, look her square in the face, and swear on the Bible I am innocent. I tell her everything the Docter say to me these past months. She cry, but I am no fool. Those tears were not for me. She only carrying on becaus her marriage vow broke.

Well, I am glad she know. She has order me to sleep in the room next to hers. Think of it! Missus herself going to protect me from her own husband.

Your daughter,
Harriet

* * *

37

Dear Mama,

I had an anxious night. I wake up to hear the Missus whisper in my ear. Then she move out of the room, but I was still afraid. And this morning she accuse me of talking to the Docter in my sleep. She dont seem to have much say-so over her feelings. Do you think she might try to hurt me?

There is now a freedom-dream in my head. John and I talk bout getting over to the big North, but never in front of Gran. She cant stand to think bout losing more family, not since Uncle Joseph run away from Mr Collins.

We dont have any money, and they watch us like spies. But John say a dream can cure a sick heart, so we plan every day.

Your H

* * *

1 November, 1828

Dear Mama,

The Docter have a new trick. You're afraid of your mistress, he say, so I will build you a small house four miles out of town. He going to set me up like a play-toy in a dollhouse. This will make a lady out of you, he claim.

The hole town know, but he is so stubborn that gossip dont stop him. Gran got the news in the street, and ask me bout it. I dont tell her how long or how bad its been. She had high words with the Docter, but her sharp tongue cant cut through his iron will.

Gran say she saw Mr Samuel Sawyer at Standin's Store. He has heared the rumors Maria Norcom been spreading about me, and he say, Aunt Molly, I am concerned for your girl. Mr Sawyer, he is a well-spoken man, and kind. He is the only one who help the poor souls been lash and left on the post at the courthouse.

Docter Norcom got no use for this Sawyer. Lass summer they had a loud falling-out right in the parlor bout some business matter. Norcom was acting his usual high-handed self, and Sawyer yell at him. Then Sawyer say he is sorry for raising his voice. But Norcom never did forget or forgive. He dont like to be crossed, especially by a younger person.

But if a White man like Sawyer be on my side, maybe the Docter will give up his idiot plan.

Your Harriet

*　*　*

2 November, 1828

Dear Mama,

The Docter gone crazy. He is sent some men out to a lonely spot to start building a cottage. But I wont never go.

I met Mr Sawyer buying tooth powder at the Market House. For a minute I think he cross Broad Street so we can meet. But that is vain! Gran say just because I am comely, dont mean I should flatter myself.

He ask bout Norcom. How does he treat you, he want to know. Does he strike or punish you? I tell him the truth. The Docter beat me with his words, I say, not his hands. But Mama, I would jump off the wharves into Edenton Bay before repeating those words out loud to a *man*!

Harriet Ann

3 November, 1828

Dear Mama,

This morning I got a note from Mr Sawyer. John, he deliver the letter and tease me when I run off to read it alone. Mr Sawyer think I am a pretty girl, Mama, and smart. It feel good to be like by an Educated gentleman! I make John swear he wont tell Gran bout the note.

Harriet

* * *

4 November, 1828

Dear Mama,

I been tossing like a dinghy all night. Mr Sawyer say, Harriet, I want to offer you my attentions. I know which attention he talking bout. Seem strange that I got to decide for my own self.

Maybe he using me to get even with old Norcom. Well, it be a way for me to get even, too. If I been with another man, the Docter might leave me alone for good. Or maybe sell me to Mr Sawyer! I got to settle on something soon, becaus that cottage going up a little higher every day.

Well, Mama, I can only tell you. I might give myself to Mr Samuel Sawyer just becaus he nice to your

Harriet Ann

* * *

5 November, 1828

Dear Mama,

After I walk back from Samuel's house, I look hard at myself in the window. Study my face to see is it change, if John or Gran can tell what I done this day. I think my eyes look older, but maybe they wont notice.

He been gentle, Mama, and make me feel special. If I cant have my sweet R, least I can be with a man who dont *own* me. I dont dare tell Gran. She like to believe I am different. Pure and untouch, she thinks. And she might say some hurtful things if she find out I need tenderness, like every other girl in this hard wurld.

Your daughter,
Harriet Ann

* * *

5 May, 1829

Dear Mama,

I been holding a lot of secret inside these lass four months. Nobody know bout Samuel except you, and even you dont know bout the baby.

Every week Norcom tell me bout progress on the cottage. I show him a blank face, so he dont know I am laughing at him on the inside. Then tonight he call me to his study. The house is finished, he say, and you must move in.

Well, I think. This going to be as satisfying as Sunday supper!

I wont never go there, I tell him.

He say, I have heard enough of such talk as that. You shall go, if you are carried by force.

I wont never go there, I say again. I be a mother in a few months.

He look like he been struck, and leave the room with out saying a word. Well, Mama, there were a few seconds of glory when I seen the look on his face. But now I feel empty. The news is out, and by sundown tomorrow everybody got to know my shame. How do I face Gran? She has keep me from harm all these years. I hope this wont make her sorry you ever had a daughter.

Harriet

* * *

9 May, 1829

Dear Mama,

Do you remember how Gran use to make horehound tea for our colds? She'd grab me by the collar and hold my nose. And I had to swallow that bitter tea or strangle. That is how I feel. Like Gran is holding me by the collar. And I am choking on bitter tears.

Gran think Norcom is the father! You are a disgrace to your dead mother, she say. Then she tear your wedding ring off my finger. Go away, she say, and dont never come to my house again!

So I walk five mile out the Soundside Road. Dont hardly know where I am going, I am crying so hard. And I lay down in a field and think bout dying. Even with a child inside me, I feel so lonesome.

Mama, I was like a baby squirrel that fall out of a tree and dont know where it is. Tree been home to the little squirrel all its life, but now home is gone. I lay there till a ram horn blow for the hands to come in from the field.

And then I remember your old friend who live nearby. So I get myself up and walk to her house.

Polly, she understand everything. But it wasn't the same as being forgive by Gran. If Gran dont love me, I think, nobody never could. Polly insist I send for her, but it was three long days before she come.

Gran sit silent when I tell her everything bout the Docter and Samuel and how I choose him becaus it seem like a way to be free. And she put her hand on my head and say, Poor child, poor child. I think Gran took pity on me, Mama, but I dont think she forgive me.

Harriet Ann

R

Dear R,

I hope you making your way in a peaceful place, hundreds of miles from here. Did you find another sweetheart to swing at a dance? When you kiss her, think bout me.

I got news both sweet and bitter. I have a Son, Joseph. His father not the one I love, but he is a feeling man and the road to freedom for me and my baby. I name the baby for my uncle, who, after six months in jail, has escape again from Mr Collins.

I am living with Gran becaus Maria Norcom don't want me back in her house. Been sickly for some time. Before the baby come I didnt leave my bed for weeks. I been half out of my mind, and had fever dreams of you and red ribbons and faces in a window. Gran sent for old Gray Head Norcom. I dont remember it, but she say I scream so hard they send him away.

Little Joseph come early and only weigh four pound. Even John want the Docter to attend the birth. He been working in the Docter's office, learning how to put up

44

medicine and to cup and bleed. Hatty, John say, the Docter know all bout bringing babies. But I refuse.

I tell him, Norcom always docter his own Slaves. He dont care bout me or the baby, he just want to save the 10 doller delivery fee. So Joseph Jacobs come into the world on Gran's feather bed with a midwife and Gran to help. I give him my father's lass name, though Daddy had no legal right to it since his daddy was White.

I am poorly and need to rest.

With much love,
Harriet

*   *   *

November, 1829

My Dear R,

Do you remember my Uncle Mark? Gran hire him out as a sailor on a packet from Edenton to New York. He is just come home with news of Uncle Joseph! Mark seen Joseph in New York City. He say he was wearing the pin I give him to remember me by. But he had little else to call his own.

Mark give him all the clothes and money he could spare. Poor Joseph. Mark say he looked sick and pale, but I think freedom will cure him. His last words to his brother were, Mark, I part with all my kin. Sorrowful words, but better to part with us than part with his life.

And Gran give me more sad news. My Aunt Betty lost another unborn child. She work too hard to carry a baby full-term! She do everything for the Norcoms. Missus say she be lost with out her, but Aunt Betty is lost all *to* her.

Make me think of you and the babies we wont never

have together. Joseph hungry. Time to put lonely thoughts and this letter away. God bless is my prayer from

Harriet Ann

*   *   *

13 August, 1831

Dear R,

Almost two years since my last letter. Being a Mama take up all my writting time. But I feel uneasy today and have a need to speak to you. There is been a strange sight in the sky this morning. The sun fade away so faint, I can look strate at it. The air got deathly still, like evil coming to call.

Then the sun turn green, and blue, and white. By afternoon it was a giant silver ball, thrown up in the sky by God or the devil him self, dont know which. People out in the street all day, staring and muttering like they afraid to speak too loud. Some of the talk saying this is the end of the wurld.

Hot as it is, Gran wont let Joseph play out on the piazza. I long to hold him close, but I got to act calm for his sake. Folk say my Son is a beautiful baby. He is a strong little boy, and call us all by name. His father come by and give him a hug ever so often. But Joseph dont know to call him Daddy.

There is something in the air. Cant say what or when, but it's on the way.

Always yours,
Harriet

*   *   *

22 August, 1831
Early morning

Dear R,

I hear whispers that there is a state of alarm from here all the way to Virginia. And every poor Slave in-betweene is in grave danger. Yesterday the Slave preacher they call Old Prophet led an army of Slaves from house to house. They has kill a lot of White folk up over the Virginia line. Some say hole families been axed to death.

Whites round here are forming patrols of men to search all the coloured quarters for more sign of rebellion. I can see them now from Gran's chamber window, pouring into town with their muskets and uniforms and drums. They say they looking for troublemakers, but what they want is revenge.

I got to get the house ready. I hope the Lord will protect Gran's home and all in it.

Your Harriet

*   *   *

Evening

Dear R,

You never heared such shouting and hollering as this mob of White folk in the street. They nothing but sorry country trash from twenty mile round. Too poor to buy Slaves of their own. So this is their great chance to climb off the bottom rung of the ladder.

They have form into groups of sixteen men headed by a captain. All day I heared the screams of Slaves being whip. The patrols swagger through the streets with clothes and anything else they got a mind to steal from the coloureds.

When they come here, we were ready. I got no weapon, so I poke them with insult instead of the barrel of a gun. Knowing signs of a decent life would pluck them, I lay Gran's best white-work quilts on the beds and put a bouquet of lavender in every room.

You remember Josiah Coffield. He is one of the meanest Slave-holders in the county. He lead the rabble in from the piazza and stand by while they tromp through the house, nosing into every drawer and trunk.

They talk biggety when they find Gran's sheets and tablecloths. Where did the damn niggers get all this? they demand. I hide my smile when Gran say, You can be sure we didnt pilfer them from *your* houses.

When they find some writting I forgot to hide away, the men hop round like they dancing barefoot on hot tin. We's got em! they yell. This here yeller gal's got letters! But their faces droop when Coffield read the letters out loud. Instead of plans to ax White people in their beds, all they heared was poems sent to me by a friend. That settled their hash!

It's getting dark now, and we have escape with out harm. I am greatful we only lost some clothing and a few jars of preserves. Like raccoons, they open the crocks and dip in their paws. But not everybody been bless this day. I still hear shrieks drifting in my window on the wicked night air.

Yours ever,
Harriet

* * *

48

12 November, 1831

Dear R,

The Slave preacher Nat Turner hung yesterday. Maybe the worst of the madness be over. Things ease up after they ketch him, but it was two month out of hell till then. Coloured folk tormented by patrols. White folk in a panic, waiting for a Slave attack. Both floors at the jail been overflowing with Slaves, and not a stick of proof against them.

Mr Small's Jim been torture till he admit he was part of a plot. But by the time they discover he make up the story, nineteen men been arrested.

In one county down south, two Slaves were suspicioned of planning a revolt. They shot them, cut off their heads, and put the heads on posts as a warning.

Here in Chowan, they not through with us yet. The prisaners been release, but there is no visiting allow betweene plantations. You know this is hard on husbands and wives who got different masters. And there are rumors if a poor White hear one note of coloured singing, he will murder the Slave before his owner can save him.

Why did they have to tear down the Slave church over in the woods? You know my dear Mama and Daddy buried there. Gran is so miserable she wont even speak of it. Whites saying now the Slaves can sit upstairs in *their* church. Remind me of a hymn the coloured folks sing: Old Satan's church is here below, up to God's free church I hope to go.

Hard times been on us, R. I am glad you not here to see it.

Harriet

January, 1833

Dear R,

I am relieve to say my family in good health. The plantations round here lost some people to cholera last September. It is a hideous disease that strike at the stomach and the bowels. Gran's friend Rachel has just succumb to rheumatic fever. The Docter been treating her for nearly two months. I will sorely miss her company, becaus she always make me laugh.

Have not been to the Norcom house since Mrs Norcom threw me out. But the Docter, he come to Gran's a few times a year to threaten me. He say if I dont give in, he going to sell my Son to a Slave-trader. I ignore him, but after each visit I grab Joseph and pull him close.

It grieve me to tell you I am expecting again. Samuel Sawyer is the father. I hope this mean freedom one day for me and my babies. Wherever you are, I know you understand. Over any other man, I wish you were their Daddy.

Always,
Harriet

* * *

October, 1833

Dear R,

My girl baptized at St. Paul's today. I did not want a christening in the White folks silk-stocking church. But Gran been attending for years, and it mean something to her.

Samuel offer to give the baby his last name. But that would only make *more* trouble. When Norcom hear about the new baby, he have a fit of anger and cut my hair close to the roots with a pair of shears. Then I talk back to old Pickle Face. Give him a piece of his own business.

R, I am greatful you were not there to see what happen next. Becaus you too tender-hearted to keep your tongue tied when the Docter hit me. Not marrying you was the rightest thing I ever decide.

Like little Joseph, my girl got the last name of her grandaddy, Daniel Jacobs. Keep me close to Daddy, somehow. His Missus from Green Hall step up at the baptism and offer her Christian name. I was too weak to say no. Make no difference anyway. A White Woman's name wont make my baby free.

Your Harriet

PART II
1835–1842

Uncle Joseph

Dear Joseph,

I remember you telling me before you run away seven years ago: Harriet, the poverty and hardship of freedom always better than Slavery. Gran, she worries that her handsome Son been living all this time like a stray dog with nowhere to go. But you made your choice. And I got to do the same.

I been asked to strike a deal with the devil. The Docter is saying he will make out free papers for my Joseph and Louisa if I move to the cottage he built for me. And I cant never see or talk to Samuel Sawyer again.

If I dont agree, Norcom going to send me and the children into plantation Slavery. Your boy shall be put to work, the Docter says, and he shall soon be sold. Your girl shall be raised for the purpose of selling well.

Last year he give the plantation to young James Norcom and his wife-to-be. You know what that means for me: like the father, so like the Son.

Free the children? Dont believe it for a minute! Unknowing to me, he'd make out false papers. There I would be, caught in his cottage, and him crowing like a chicken riding a horse.

Well, I have made me a plan. I feel strong when I recall what you said in jail: We dont die but once.

Harriet

* * *

April, 1835
Auburn plantation

Dear Joseph,

First time in six years I been away from your good mama's safe home. Louisa and I ride out here last week in an old steer cart. Little Joseph feeling puny, so they let him stay with Gran.

At least we're not in the fields, though I been working like a mule since I got here. Young master wants me to wait on him in the great house, so Louisa and I, we sleep in a little room on the third floor. Sometimes it is a heavy load, carrying Lulu up those thirty-seven stairs at the end of a day.

Got no time to spend with my baby girl. She wanders round alone, and when I hear her crying, makes my own eyes sting. I am getting the house ready for young James and his bride. Cleaned the carpets and all the drapes, then started to making sheets, tablecloths, and towels. But while I sew, my mind moves quick as my fingers.

Joseph, I need a good dose of your nerve and Mama's patience. If my plan goes well, the Docter going to sell the children fast as lightning. And he wont even know they been bought by their Daddy.

Harriet

* * *

Early May, 1835

Dear Joseph,

Louisa had a close call a few days ago. Crawled out from under the house, and a fat snake come slithering out after her. The young master killed it, but he feel guilty.

It was easy to talk him into sending her back to Gran. She went to town yesterday in an old cart filled with shingles. Young James says ugly words bout coloured children being broke in, but I guess he is too young yet to be hard as his Daddy.

I had a scare, too. My arms aching to hold little Joseph, so I creep away in the middle of the night. One of the Norcom field hands lead me on the six-mile walk through the woods to town. There was a big yellow moon. It remind me of my first dance and make me feel like a young girl.

I climb in Gran's bedchamber window and steal a few prised minutes with the family by moonlight. My heart was so full when I see them all that I just stand there and cry. Then my friend, he come back all too soon for the return trip.

Three miles out we hear the pattyrollers, and for a few awful seconds we listen for the dogs. Thank God they leave their bloodhounds at home that night. We just had time to hide behind a great oak tree before they come fast by, drinking and partying.

My guide says sometimes he leaves vines tied across the road to nock the poor White pecks off their horses. And if dogs chasing you, he tells me, grease the bottom of your feet with snuff and lard. Then they lose the scent. Makes me trembly to think of that, Joseph. But I will be bold like you, and get ready for the worst.

Harriet A

* * *

24 May, 1835
Sunday

Dear Joseph,

Today is my chance. They letting me spend Sabbath with Gran. She been my faithful old companion, and being with her is a comfort. Here is the plan: I will hide in the house of a friend. Then Norcom, he'll think I escaped to the Free States. So he will sell little Joseph and Louisa to be rid of them, and Samuel can buy his children.

I talk to Mama and Daddy at the burying ground this evening. Mama's tree only a black stump now, and the letters on Daddy's marker been weathered away. But I never felt closer to them, not even when writting them letters.

I kneel down in the dark woods, Joseph, and I pray for help. And when I pass the poor wrecked coloured church, seem like Daddy's voice come from it, strong as ever. Hurry on, Harriet, he tells me. Hurry till you get to freedom or the grave!

Harriet J

* * *

Dear Joseph,

My courage has leave me. Gran, she beg me not to go. Nobody respects a mother who leaves her children, she says, and you going to make me miserable the short time I got left to live.

She remind me how they parade you through the town in chains when you were caught the first time. She is bent over with her sixty-five years, Joseph. I cant add more weight to the load.

I need a new scheme. But James Norcom is married Wednesday. And there is so many chores to do I cant think strate till after the wedding.

Harriet

* * *

6 June, 1835
11 P.M.

Dear Joseph,

I am leaving tonight at twelve. But time hangs on like a dead branch that wont fall. My chair is pull to the open window—the air in this little room is stifling. Between heat and fear, I cant catch my breath.

The marriage last week stick like grit in my craw. They had a wedding dinner, and for the first time ever I had to wait round a table. But the worst was seeing the Docter and his wife. I had not seen her face-to-face for five years. And I can tell by the way she turn up the corners of her mouth, I am just where she wants me: serving her family and miles from her house back in town.

Today she and the Docter come visiting. And I overhear the Docter say to his Son, Dont wait any longer, send for them tomorrow! I know what their plan is. They think they so clever to bring my children back to the farm to be broke in like animals. Long as Joseph and Louisa are here, the Norcoms know I wont never run. But I am one step ahead.

Midnight. Three times you escaped, Uncle Joseph. Send me some of your daring! I need it to slip down these creaky stairs and climb out into the dark night.

H A

* * *

7 June, 1835
The house of a friend

Dear Joseph,

I run the six miles to Gran's house like a scalded cat. Thoughts of pattyrollers and dogs circling round my head the whole time. The Woman who rents a room from Gran raised her window when I whisper, Sally, I have run away! Let me in, quick.

She opens the door and begs me not to leave. Mister Sawyer been here last week, she says softly. He told Molly he will help her buy you and the children. Dont run away, Harriet, she says. Your grandmama all bowed down with trouble now.

But I was out of time. Samuel always been big on promises, but what good are they when my Son and daughter going to the plantation in only a few hours? I ask her to hide my clothes in her trunk, then I kiss my sleeping babies good-bye. Doubts pour over me. They got no true father, and now they got no Mama.

By sunrise, I guess young James finds I am gone. Becaus by ten o'clock, the Docter come and tear up every inch of Gran's house. My trunk was empty, so all day they been searching ships, thinking I'm headed North. My friend has hide me well. She just come back with a notice she tore off the courthouse door. The Docter, he is wasted no time posting this broadside for miles round:

$300 REWARD! Ran away from the subscriber, an intelligent, bright, mulatto girl, named Harriet, 21 years of age. Five feet four inches high. Dark eyes, and black hair inclined to curl; but it can be made straight. Has a decayed spot on a front tooth. She can read and write, and in all probability will try to get to the Free States. All persons are forbidden, under penalty of law, to harbor or employ said Slave. $150 will be given to whoever takes her in the state, and $300 if taken out of the state and delivered to me, or lodged in jail.

DR. NORCOM

My friend says there is a night watch for me over the town. But she brung glad news, too. When she tells me my children still safe at Gran's, we cry together like folks at a camp meeting. So the plan is worked! The hound is too busy hunting the fox to take Joseph and Louisa to the farm. But now the War is on.

Harriet Ann J

* * *

61

Dear Joseph,

Days of watching and waiting. I remember your months in the jail, covered with lice. Sometimes nothing but white beans and water to eat. How come you stood it so long?

I been sending messages to Gran and Mark. I tell them I am safe, but make sure they dont know where. They send messages back, begging me to return. Ask the master's forgiveness, they say, and let him make an example of you.

And what would that be? Bent over in the cotton fields with a sack hanging from my neck to the ground? Hands ripped after twelve hours of picking cotton bolls?

Or would he insist on a public whipping, like Mr Collins wanted to give you, Uncle? I think of the poor Slaves on the post behind the courthouse. The lash hissing through the air like cold water on a red-hot iron. If I have to die first, that memory wont never ride my children at night.

Harriet

*   *   *

15 June, 1835

Dear Joseph,

The pain is awful. Last night a search patrol come very near my hiding spot. So I fly out in a panic and hide in a thicket of bushes for two hours. I was like a turtle, afraid to move. Then something cold and slimy grabbed my leg. I slap at the thing, but it was too dark to see if it was a snake.

When I limp back to the house, my leg is already

swelled from the poisonous bite. I tell my friend, Pack it with warm ashes and vinegar, then run to the root Docter. Soak a dozen copper pennies in vinegar overnight, root Docter says, and use the vinegar as a dressing in the morning.

The pain has let up some, but it is hard to walk. And Gran has send a message. Leave this house at nine tonight. Go to the back side of the warehouse down at the water. I be meeting somebody, dont know who. Going someplace, dont know where. Joseph, feels like I am walking blindfolded strate into the bay.

H A Jacobs

*   *   *

16 June, 1835

Dear Joseph,

I did not drown in the bay and go to heaven. But I am in the house of an angel! With light flooding my room. And I lay here on a pile of feather beds, just like some queen from the Bible. My belly is still full from the hot supper I eat last night: pork stew, sweet white corn, and buttered biscuit. Best of all, I been spying on the Docter from the window when he marches down Broad Street to his office.

Well, I went to the warehouse like I been told. Nobody much round, but I know the night patrols be looking for me soon, because it is almost dark. Nothing left of daylight but purple streaks across the sky. I squat like a rat behind a barrel, my leg hot and throbby. And Joseph, I am scared down to my toes.

Then soft footsteps come down the path, and a low voice called my name: Harriet! I almost hollered when I see my old friend, Luna, who is cook for the Widow Blount. She dont say another word, but hurried me along to the Widow's house.

When we were inside, she says, Honey, now you safe. The devils aint coming to search *this* house. I expect you need some supper after all this scaring.

Luna, she says that yesterday Gran told Martha Blount all my troubles. Gran been knowing her for years because the Widow, she related to Elizabeth Horniblow. And Missus Blount says, Aunt Molly, I will hide Harriet. But you must swear you will never mention my name, or it would ruin me and my family.

And that is how I am in this storeroom at the top of the stairs, right over the Missus' bedchamber. Except for Luna and her husband, not even Miss Blount's other coloured people know I am here. So, Uncle, I have won the first battle in this War.

Harriet

* * *

17 June, 1835

Dear Joseph,

It is only Martha Blount who has keep me from flying out of the house to the jail. Less than three blocks from this cosey room, John, Aunt Betty, and my children sit behind thick flat bars on a cold stone floor. You will never see them again, Norcom tells Gran, not till Harriet is brought back.

Luna brung a message from John: Wherever you are, dont come here. We be much better off than you are. If you come you going to ruin us all. They would force you to tell where you been, or kill you.

So Martha Blount has talk me into staying. She says Aunt Betty will take good care of Joseph and Louisa. Poor Aunt Betty. Only crime she commit is loving us too much.

Uncle, I see a picture in my mind. Six years ago. Midnight. Me and Gran, we dress up in dark clothes to sneak a visit to you in the jail. The cell is quiet as death, and the moon is watching us through the bars. I hear the rattle of chains and soft crying when Gran warms your cold hands in hers.

I put my babies in that picture. Then I squeeze my eyes shut tight to make it disappear.

H Ann

* * *

17 July, 1835

Dear Joseph,

After a month, Aunt Betty is let out of jail. Guess it is too tiring for Mrs Norcom to fix her own dinner and eat it, too. Luna goes to see John and the children, and I weep after each visit. She says John holds them up to the grated window and they prattle on bout their Mama.

Had a great fright a few days ago. Norcom stops by Gran's and tells her he knows where I am. Says he will have me by midnight. Gran and Mark got word to Luna. She rush me down the stairs, across the yard, and into the kitchen.

I wiggle down into a hollow space under the floor-boards. It was padded with a buffalo skin and a scrap of carpet to lie on. Luna, she lays the plank down and I got just enough room to bring my hands to my face. I been bit by a small snake, I think, and chased by a big one. Now these reptiles going to walk on top of me.

Stay there, Luna says, till I see do they know bout you— if they *did* know where you are, they wont know *now*.

But it was all a trick. While the other housmaids walk across the kitchen floor, nocking dirt into my eyes and mouth, Luna tells stories bout me to draw them out. They are sure I am in the North by now. Philadelphia, or New York, they say. Word travels fast round the kitchens of Edenton. Some folks call it the Black Dispatch. If the Docter suspicioned my whereabouts, the housmaids would know.

When they went to bed, Luna raised the plank. Come out, child, she says. They dont know nothing bout you. 'Twas only White folks lies, to scare us niggers. Well. The lies done their work.

H J

* * *

15 August, 1835

Dear Joseph,

Two months and my family still in prisan. Norcom come to this house today and I almost faint when I hear him downstairs. Cant make out the words, but I surely know his preachy-sounding voice. Luna tells me he come to borrow 500 doller from Martha Blount to chase after me in New York.

But he will waste her money and his time. Luna and Martha Blount both saying he is discouraged. Now is the time for Mister Sawyer to buy your children, they say.

I got word for Gran to talk to Samuel, but I dont hold

much hope. Norcom is aggravated. He needs my babies to work out his spite on me.

Harriet A

* * *

18 August, 1835

Dear Joseph,

I have bit my lips till they bloody. I overhear two housmaids this morning. One says yesterday a speculator bought John and the children. The other maid says No, the Daddy is bought them.

Last night I feel in my bones that something has happen. I hear singing outside the window. Then the singing turn into the moans of Joseph and Louisa. I know it sounds strange to you, Uncle, but you not a Mama. When I kneel down to pray, my children pass in front of me, like spirit ships out on the ocean.

If Luna dont get up here soon, I—

* * *

Evening

Dear Joseph,

I almost forget what *happy* is! Luna come to say the children and John now belong to Samuel. They is taken their first step to freedom. And what a jig they dance for Norcom!

Here is Luna's report: Early yesterday, Samuel sends a Slave-trader to offer 900 doller for John and 800 for Joseph and Louisa. Being short on money, Norcom demands 1900 for them all. The trader, he agrees, but he insists that the sale be quick. He got a drove of Slaves to get out of town, he says, and have to be on his way. By ten o'clock, John and the children were in his hands.

A blacksmith fix a Slave-chain forty feet long with handcuffs every two or three feet. The men were tightly chain together, like peppers threaded on a string. Then come the children in a cart, and the Women walking behind.

You seen it before, Luna tells me. Husbands sold from they wives like bulls from cows, children torn from they Mama's arms. The speculator, says Luna, and shakes her head. He buys cheap and sells high.

She says Norcom wearing a satisfied look when he watch this mournful parade leave town. I guess he was thinking my family wont never annoy him again. But Samuel and the Slave-trader, they has made a deal. The trader stops at Mr Skinner's farmhouse a few miles out and hammers off John's irons.

My brother somehow finds a wagon and takes Joseph and Louisa back to Gran's. Luna waiting there, too. She says Gran quick close the curtains and light the candles. She hugs her great-grandbabies, then falls on her knees to give thanks.

John grabs the children, Luna tells me with a grin on her face, and they dance in a circle, laughing and shouting. And I am only a few blocks away, unknowing what all is happening to them I love best in the world. Well, their Mama wasn't there to watch them celebrate, but their Daddy was.

Samuel shows up after dark, Luna says, looking pleased with what is happen. Well, Uncle, he never done nothing against our children. But till now, little for them, either. Seeing them so happy, maybe he is thinking bout setting them free. But I wont hope for too much at once. For now, the dark cloud of my life has roll away.

At peace,
Harriet

* * *

19 August, 1835

Dear Joseph,

Another day buried under the floor. Didnt take the Docter long to find out who *did* buy his Slaves, and now he is stirred up again. Gran's house been search every day. Docter accuses Mark of helping me escape and is put him in jail.

So when Luna gets word of the searching, she hides me again. Patrols were all over the house, thick as hairs on a man's head, she says. Under the boards, I can hear their rude voices and feel them clomping over my head.

I cant stay here, Uncle, it's too dangerous for everybody. Besides, I am sick from laying on the damp ground in one spot. I cant go back down in that hole again.

Norcom threaten Gran. If I meet John in the street, he say, I'll flog him within an inch of his life! So Samuel thinks John would be safer if he works on his farm for a few months.

Luna is seen the children today. They a little puny from two months in jail, she says, but will be muley strong soon.

Harriet Ann

* * *

Dear Joseph,

It is nearbout dark. I write with the sound of water slap-slapping against the ship. Do you remember when you sang and laughed in jail, till Mister Collins had you ironed? Praise God, you cant see me now, dressed in a pea jacket and trousers and my hair tucked under a tarpaulin hat. Your laughing would give us all away.

I am in great danger. Yesterday I was sewing by the window and waiting for my evening treat: watching Norcom walk home from his office. Then I hear a key rattling in the storeroom door. The needle freezes in my hand, and I hear more keys. But none fit, and there is a faint rustle of skirts as footsteps fall away. When Luna bring my supper, I tell her what is happen.

I know who it is, says she. Depend upon it, that was Jenny. She always got the devil in her! She just want to find out who have cut and make my new gown. I'll get Missus to fix her, Luna says.

But then we look at each other. And we both know my safe time here at Martha Blount's house is over. When she tells the Missus, Missus says to keep Jenny busy in the kitchen while she goes to see Mark. And now he and Gran has arrange a new hiding place for me.

Luna says, I'm so glad you going to free parts! Dont forget old Luna, perhaps I'll come along by and by. Then she gives me this sailor suit. Put your hands in your pockets, she says, and walk ricketty, like the sailors. And with a buckeye in my pocket for good luck, I leave the two good Women who risked their lives for me.

When I walk outside, the fresh air smells so fine I almost

forget to be scared. Peter is my guide—a trusty man who used to work with Daddy. Be brave, he whispers, I got a dagger.

I thought bout you wandering the streets of Baltimore, Uncle, when you were too sick to keep up your escape. And how you run smack into a White man from Edenton! For a runaway Slave, walking round town feels like walking round naked. Seem like everybody was staring right at me. But I guess this sailor look like all the others in town, except a little shorter.

Aunt Betty's good husband, Uncle Stephen, meet us at the wharf and row us out to his owner's empty ship. And here we sit all night like ducks. At dawn we be leaving the ship because the patrols might search it for runaways. Then Uncle Stephen going to row us over to the Snaky Swamp. And there we sit some more, till he come back to get us at dusk.

Joseph, I look down in these waters and remember you almost took your own life after your first capture. Like you, only thinking bout the family keeps me from pitching myself over the side.

Harriet

*   *   *

23 August, 1835

Dear Joseph,

Two days in the swamp has give me a roaring fever. We are back on the ship for a third night. But Peter swears, Harriet, I will take you home even if the devil himself is on patrol. What home? I think, I got no home now.

There is more snakes in the swamp than God can count,

and enough mosquitoes to make a pie. Peter hacked out a place in the briers and brambles for me to sit, but by sundown, we had to beat the snakes away from our feet with sticks.

I am hot and cold all at once, and my head feels light as cotton. Peter says Uncle Mark been working on a new hiding place, and Uncle Stephen be rowing us back to the wharf. Blacken your face with charcoal, he is telling me now, and get ready to walk two blocks to your grand-mother's house.

Peter's voice sounds sad, Uncle Joseph. You got to make the most of this walk, he says, because you wont get another very soon.

Harriet

Uncle Stephen

September, 1835

Dear Stephen,

It is hard to breathe in here, the air is so close and stale. Makes me feel like I been buried alive. I think of you out at sea, and remember what you tell Aunt Betty once when you come home from a trip: Bet, you say, I belong to Mister B and I work his ship. But when we sailing along, I am free as a bluebird!

This hiding place reminds me of a sailor's bed. The space is only nine feet long and seven feet wide. The high part is three feet, then it slopes down to nothing. But I dont feel like any bluebird. More like a dressed chicken, ready for the spit.

Being sick with fever, I dont remember my first days here, and that is merciful. Gran and Mark helped me stand on a barrel to climb through the trapdoor. I sleep for hours and hours on a bed of blankets, unknowing that mice run over me.

Under my blankets are rough boards that make the ceiling of the room under me. Five years ago, Uncle Mark built a storeroom on the piazza for Gran's barrels of flour and meal. While I was in the Snaky Swamp, he quick built a cupboard in the corner of the storeroom. Then he cut a hole through the top of the cupboard into my space. When not being used to pass messages or food, the trapdoor fits back into place. It is my door to the world.

The heat was bad at first. There is only thin pine shingles between me and the sun. And after the heat come the red mites. Hundreds of little tiny insects no bigger than the point of a hemming needle. They poke into my skin and burn like sparks from Gran's oven. She give me cold tea compresses. After some weeks, the sting went away.

Today was a small victory. I hit my head on a gimlet that Mark forgot and left stuck in the wall. So I use the gimlet to drill three little holes, one above the other. Then I make holes between the holes, till I got a peephole one inch long and one inch broad. I been sitting by it for hours, taking in as much fresh air as I can.

Sometimes, Uncle Stephen, I think I might start to holler and never stop.

                                            Harriet

                    *   *   *

                                    October, 1835
Dear Uncle Stephen,

This is the truth from my heart, from here to glory: I dont blame you, and I hope you dont blame Yourself. From where I sit, I say freedom is worth any price. But I am sorry the price you got to pay is never seeing Aunt Betty again.

Gran whispers through the trapdoor last night that Betty is beside herself. When Mister B's ship come home with out you yesterday, she almost faint dead away. She is full of grief, and I wish I could go to her.

But nobody knows I'm up here, except Gran and Uncle Mark. When Norcom put Mark in jail, he threatened to torture him to find out where I was. So, to protect Betty, they wont tell her till it's safe. And the children, they cant never suspect their Mama is a-laying up under the roof in a space no bigger than a few coffins.

I can hear Joseph and Louisa playing only a few feet away on the piazza. And if I hold myself just right, I can look through the peephole and see the street. Some mornings I even see the Docter on his way to the office. He just spent good money looking for me again in New York. After separating you from Aunt Betty, I can guess how you feel bout him, Stephen.

It's all my doing, Uncle, and that cuts me up inside. Norcom was trying to punish *me* when he forbid Betty to see you after I run away. You been a loyal friend. I wont soon forget that you risked the lash, hiding me on your master's ship. And you'd have found me passage to the North if there'd been any safe way to do it. Aunt Betty lost a treasure when she lost you, and it's all my fault.

It's raining some now. The damp air cools the boards under my back. Takes my mind off feeling like I am the only person left in the world.

Harriet

* * *

November, 1835

Dear Uncle Stephen,

All the years I been reading the newspaper, I never did think I would see my own name. Aunt Betty found this old copy laying in the Docter's study and give it to Gran. I scraped some drops of pine tar from the shingles to stick the notice here in my book.

$100 REWARD

WILL be given for the apprehension and delivery of my Servant Girl HARRIET. She is a light mulatto, 21 years of age, about 5 feet 4 inches high, of a thick and corpulent habit, having on her head a thick covering of black hair that curls naturally, but which can be easily combed straight. She speaks easily and fluently, and has an agreeable carriage and address. Being a good seamstress, she has been accustomed to dress well, has a variety of very fine clothes, made in the prevailing fashion, and will probably appear, if abroad, tricked out in gay and fashionable finery. As this girl absconded from the plantation of my son without any known cause or provocation, it is probable she designs to transport herself to the North.

The above reward, with all reasonable charges, will be given for apprehending her, or securing her in any prison or jail within the U. States.

All persons are hereby forewarned against haboring or entertaining her, or being in any way instrumental in her escape, under the most rigorous penalties of the law.

JAMES NORCOM.

Edenton, N. C. June 30

John is moved back to town from the Sawyer farm. He is to be Samuel's personal servant in his town house, and to check on Samuel's Brother and sister. They need watching, since they both subject to fits. So John got a long-time pass to be out late. Some nights he lifts my trapdoor and we talk in whispers.

He says his lot is better now. He eats enough and there is no threat of the whip. But John still has his freedom-dream. He says, Harriet, I am only happier because I can see my chance for escape clearer.

When we were little, I was Miss High-and-Mighty. I always thought John be the one to get in trouble. Now John out walking in the fresh air. And look at me, a-laying up here like a bird with a broken wing.

Uncle Mark is made one small improvement. His chamber is on the house side of my cell. He nock a hole through the plaster wall behind his bed. They have to kneel down and lean over, but now I can talk to him and Gran more easy.

The weather in October was bearable, but come November there was an early frost. Gran brung more covers and heated bricks, but with out the fireplace, I am helpless against the cold.

It has warm up some the past few days. I am planning what to make for Joseph and Louisa for Christmas. I thank God for knowing how to sew. Not in the mood to thank Miss Margaret.

Harriet

* * *

25 December, 1835

Dear Uncle Stephen,

We have had no strate news of you. Aunt Betty still broke up over you running away, but mostly she is strong bout it, like when she lose your babies year after year.

Sometimes she cries and says she never even got to say good-bye. When my arms and legs get so cramped I cant hardly move, I try to remember others suffering besides me.

I hope you celebrating your first free Christmas in a warm, safe spot. But wherever you are, you missing a feast. All day I been smelling Gran's roast turkey and pork. Gran, she cooks Christmas dinner up right, with stewed vegetables, oyster soup, and her best fruitcake. After dark, she will tap on a certain wall, that means food coming.

It is a lonely business, spending Christmas in this dark hole. My children so close by I can hear them playing with the dolls I made. And Joseph, what a proud little man he is, walking round in the suit I sewed. Well, they not with their Mama, but they not in the Slave quarters at Auburn. When it gets dreadful bad, I think of that.

Gran is invited an odd crew to dinner: the town constable and a free coloured—a traitor who puts himself in a good light with White folks by catching runaways like me. She plans to take them upstairs and show them Uncle Mark's pet mockingbird. Then they can see for themselves: nobody hiding in Molly Horniblow's house.

I been reading the Bible many hours a day. I'm not sure there is a Promised Land, but it helps to pretend.

Harriet

*　*　*

Dear Uncle Stephen,

I dont always recall what day it is. Sometimes I sleep for hours in fits and starts, hardly knowing who or where I am. Then it gets dark and Gran nocks to bring food or empty the slop bucket. And I wake up cold and stiff and wondering why God lets Maria Norcom sleep in a feather bed while I sleep on boards.

Lately it's been too noisy to pass the hours sleeping. They is making repairs to the courthouse roof, and the hammering and clinking travels easy through the cold winter air. Hours and hours of it, till the sound bores into my head the way those mites got into my skin.

There was two inches of snow a few weeks back. I heard my boy and girl outside, playing and squealing like two little pigs. Gran puts Joseph in charge of his little sister, the way she used to put me in charge of John. Except Joseph not as bossy as me.

Last week a heavy rain come, Gran said the worst in a year. Uncle Mark give me oakum to fill in the chinks between the shingles. Even so, my clothes soak through, like I been baptize in the creek. Gran been bringing me hot sassafras tea, hoping I wont get sick. Nobody to docter me if I do, except John.

Samuel's been sending John out to the Sawyer plantation to treat his coloureds. The overseer, he always claims they not sick, but John goes right on giving Peru-bark for the mittent fever and mullen and onion syrup for the cough. Aunt Betty says Norcom is well-known for his doctering. I guess he taught John well. But how can a man

79

good at healing a body have so little care for the spirit inside?

Gran says there is been smallpox over in Elizabeth City. Lord, save us.

Harriet

* * *

August, 1836

Dear Uncle Stephen,

Your poor Betty been plagued all summer. It was a sickly season, and she is nursed everybody in the Norcom house. One of the Docter's young boys, Standin, had the cold and fever. Their infant Son, William, got it next. Not much help from Maria Norcom—she gone out to Auburn to nurse young James's little Martha.

Many of Norcom's coloured folks been bad, too. Melah lost her little girl. Gran, she thinks it might be cholera.

She frets bout me, but I say, Gran, I am too mean to get sick. The heat been fierce, till thick tears of turpentine fall from the roof. It gets in my hair and no amount of combing will unstick it. It's so hot under these boards even the mosquitoes dont visit. When I forgive God enough to pray, I thank Him for that small favor.

Gran and Mark still looking for an escape route. But Norcom has the ships searched now and again. The risk of running is too high, especially when it means leaving my babies to try it.

Thinking back, Stephen, I wonder that you waited so long to escape. Many a time, you could have hop ship at a Northern port. But for twenty years you keep coming back to your Bet. She thinks becaus you were marry regular by a preacher. But I think because you loved your wife more than freedom. Aunt Betty, she was blessed.

Harriet

*   *   *

December, 1836

Dear Uncle Stephen,

Christmas already. Time is a whisper I cant hear. Was it yesterday I watch my little boy riding through the yard on a cornstalk horse? And Louisa, she was rocking her muslin baby with the button eyes. But that was last week! Yes, I remember clear now. There were copper-colored leaves falling past the peephole.

We had a hard rain, then snow, then more rain. I am cold, so cold.

Harriet

*   *   *

January, 1837

Dear Uncle Stephen,

Uncle, I nearly died. John found me a-laying in a stupor. I come to with him throwing water in my face and crying over and over, Harriet, wake up! My head, face, even my tongue, turn numb. For weeks he been nursing me with herbs, roots, and ointment. Today I can sit up a little to write this letter, but only to tell you that Gran is now broke down her self.

I take the blame. All the worry been too much for her. Some of the silver-spoon ladies in town been visiting Gran. Maria Norcom, she dont bend her head for nobody.

But she was shamed by the others into coming by. First thing out of her brass-spoon mouth was, Mark, why havent you called for Docter Norcom!

So she sends for the Docter strate away, and I have a fit of panic when I hear him downstairs. He has offer his services, but Mark thinks he only wants to run up a bill. The Norcoms, they are two limbs from the same tree. And neither gives a twig for Gran.

I hope prayer is enough to get her well. Luna would say, If you let a buzzard spread the shadow of his wings on the roof, death will come. But Gran dont hold with superstition. The Lord put me in this world, she says, and He can take me out.

Harriet

* * *

1 August, 1837

Dear Uncle Stephen,

Sickness finally left this house. I guess somebody wipe the buzzard's shadow off the roof. Gran is well again, and I thank God for that. It is been intensely hot. I am ashamed to say I spend most hours wearing only a chemise and underwearing.

The town is dull and lifeless. I dont hear people calling to each other in the street, even by midmorning. Aunt Betty says all the White folks gone to New Bern to breathe the healthy sea air. But I know one White folk gone North again, looking for his valuable property.

When Gran tells me the Docter went to New York, I feel safer right off. So early in the morning I been climbing down to the storeroom and stretching my arms and legs.

When they help me down the first time, I sway like a sapling in the wind, then my ankles give way.

The door to the storeroom got windows in it. When I can stand, I look out and fill my eyes with the dawn till Gran whispers, Harriet, the children be waking up soon.

Aunt Betty says Norcom coming back in time to vote on August 10. Samuel is running for Congress. Uncle, I dont dare think of the election. What if he wins and goes to Washington City with out freeing the children? What if he dies and the children, they sold away?

Well, Gran says a lot of what-ifs dont make a did-happen. I got ten days to figure it out, and I been learning something bout patience.

Harriet

* * *

September, 1837

Dear Uncle Stephen,

You and Aunt Betty lost a sluice of babies. But if you'd raised any you'd understand how anxious I been. Gran and Mark all put out with me, and even your sweet Betty says I been foolish.

Yesterday Mark tells me Samuel is taking the night steamboat to Washington City. Guess he thinks he is going to be a big boss-dog politician. With out telling anybody, I climb down to the storeroom at nine o'clock. My legs limp, like baby-doll legs. Had to sit on the floor and smack them to get the blood rolling again.

I have not been so scared since the first night you hide me on Mister B's ship. Soon I hear Samuel on the street. He tells his friend, Wait here, I've got to see Aunt Molly.

Then he visits with Gran and says good-bye to Joseph and Louisa. Reckon he feels like a Daddy sometimes, even if he dont act it out in public.

When he walks back out, I grab my chance. Stop a minute, I say real low through the half-open shutter, and let me speak for my babies. Imagine how I feel, Stephen, when he keeps on going and I hear the gate slam. But presently he come back after sending the friend on his way.

Who called me? he asks.

I did, I reply.

Harriet! says he. I knew your voice, but I was afraid to answer. They are mad to allow you to hide here!

I dont want nothing for myself, I whisper. All I ask is you free the children before you go.

I will free them, Samuel promises, and I shall try again to purchase you from Docter Norcom. Stephen, I *heard* him say the words. But even as I write them down, they hard to believe.

Then Samuel goes inside and tells Gran not to let me stay in her house overnight, or we will all be caught. He would not believe the truth if he heard it: that I been here for two years. And in that time, only two things left in my life's cup: the pain in my body and the sound of my children growing up.

Gran and Mark helped me back up to the hole in the dark. Come, come, child, she fussed, it wont do for you to stay down here another minute. You've done wrong, she said, but I cant blame you. Mark brung me hot flag-root tea to ease the hurting in my legs. Then he left me alone with only my letters to you.

Harriet

84

2 January, 1838

Dear Uncle Stephen,

A quiet Christmas season. Not even a gunshot or fire-cracker at the New Year. The only bright decoration been the Johnkannaus parade. This year some coloured hands come across the Sound from Mr Collins's Somerset plantation. They join up with the rest of the gang, and I heard them singing and prancing up Broad Street.

A few Womenfolk come, too, and Gran got to visit with her old friends Violet and Betsy. She serve tea and some fresh-baked rusks. Even pull out her snowy white cloths and silver teaspoons from the buffet. To hear them laughing and talking all at once was a gift.

Your Bet come to see me last night. She always feels poorly at the end of Hiring-Out Day. Says she needs to be with her own family after seeing so many others broke up. She says even the Docter acting low.

This is an unhappy country! she heard the Docter tell his wife, in which man is obliged to tax his fellow man for sweat and service against his will.

Stephen, that's big talk. But Norcom, he dont feel bad *enough*. Else he'd do all the tilling and planting and hoeing and cleaning his own self, and let us go free. But Slavery must be like that claret he likes to drink. It's just too good to give up.

Harriet

* * *

85

10 January, 1838

Dear Uncle Stephen,

I been passing many hours sewing pieces of dresses and shirts that Gran cut out. And my brain is busy as the needle. What if Norcom thought for sure I was in the North? Then I could feel safer, like I did when he gone looking for me last summer.

Well, Stephen. Your Betty always says, You dont get nowhere a-setting on your hands. And I been getting plenty of practice writing letters. Now I'm ready to cut up some meanness!

Harriet

* * *

20 January, 1838
Sullivan Street
New York City

Dear Docter Norcom,

Do you remember your Harriet? You knew me when I was a child and helpless in your power. Years of misery you brung to me. Now I am free of you and doing well here in the Free States.

You will be glad to know I still wear fine clothes and got a good head of thick hair. My friends say I look quite healthy.

Please do me the favor of delivering the sealed letter to my grandmother. And give my regards to your kind wife.

Believe me,
Very truly
No longer yours,
Harriet Ann Jacobs

*　*　*

20 January, 1838

Dear Grandmother,

This letter will be delivered to you by favor of Docter
Norcom. Can you send Joseph and Louisa to me as soon
as possible? I need them with me, as in the North I can
teach them to respect themselves.

I am now with friends in New York, but live in Boston.
Please send your answer to 31 Atkinson Street, Boston,
Massachusetts.

Your affectionate
Harriet

*　*　*

21 January, 1838

Dear Uncle Stephen,

Gran says Norcom going to figure out my trick and nock
hell's pete out of the children just to get even. But it's
more of a risk for Peter, who is fixed it so the letter be
mailed from New York.

I would trade Mama's silver thimble just to see Norcom
go chasing after me in Boston.

Harriet

*　*　*

24 January, 1838

Dear Uncle Stephen,

The bluff have done its work. Aunt Betty told Gran that
Norcom got the letters. Gran expecting him to come and
leaves the door open downstairs so I can hear them talking.

He come in with my letters, Gran says, his eyes bright as blue glass marbles.

She sits him in a chair near the door. I suppose, Molly, he says, you have no objection to my reading the letter Harriet has written to you. And then he reads his made-up letter from me:

Dear Grandmother, it said. *I have long wanted to write to you, but the disgraceful manner in which I left you and my children made me ashamed to do it. I have purchased freedom at a dear rate. If any arrangement could be made for me to return to the South with out being a Slave, I would gladly come. Write as soon as possible to your unhappy granddaughter.   Harriet*

Old Gray Head, he thinks he can trick Gran into getting me back home. Well, it proves he believes I am in the North, and that is been my aim all along. Now I can climb down to the storeroom every day.

Harriet

*   *   *

July, 1838

Dear Uncle Stephen,

John been sent to Washington City to serve Samuel. His letters say life for a Slave is better there. He can come and go all he wants, and there is lots of lively parties and carryings-on. Says the men in Congress play cards as much as they vote.

Ever since my Brother left, I been thinking bout his freedom-dream. Be so easy for him to slip away. Samuel promised John, You'll never serve another master after me. It's a good thing promises are free, or Samuel would be in the poorhouse. He is lied something scandalous, Uncle Stephen. Been almost a year, and Joseph and Louisa not free yet.

Harriet

* * *

Dear Uncle Stephen,

John is written to say that Samuel will be married next month. She is the niece of the Woman who runs his boardinghouse in Washington City. The wedding will be in Chicago and John going with them. I been cheated all round. My children losing their Daddy and maybe their freedom. I am losing the onliest White man I ever felt safe with. And Chicago is in a Free State. Might lose my Brother, too.

Harriet

* * *

22 July, 1838

Dear Uncle Stephen,

I cant worry bout anything but the heat now. Aunt Betty heard Norcom complain it was one hundred degrees in his office. Sometimes I think I am ready to go to my glory.

Then I hear the children on the piazza and I forget myself for a while. An exhibit come through town last Saturday, and Gran says everybody threw down work to go. The whole county was there. Even Docter Norcom with his young children, laughing at the animals in spite of his sour self.

Gran, she says Joseph and Louisa were happy as two birds flying, and didn't seem to notice the strong smell of the beasts or their dung. But she almost choke on the stench. She is a good soul to do this for my motherless babies.

Harriet

* * *

11 August, 1838

Dear Uncle Stephen,

The heat is not let up. There is a drought, and Aunt Betty says Norcom's crops are half gone. Death been dancing through town: They found Charles, a coloured boy, drowned at the mouth of Queen Anne's Creek. And Norcom's Son, Benjamin Rush, is dying of a slow and painful disease.

Samuel being married today. John wrote that they taking him with them on their honeymoon to Canada. Most likely they having a fancy-hat wedding in a big church with flowers, and a cake all iced up white as snow. No jumping like a cricket over a broomstick for Samuel's lady. No, sir.

Only the best for Miss Lavinia. I never met her, but how come it I know, Uncle Stephen, she is just a loaf of sugar no bigger than a button, with cheeks as pink as an apple blossom, and little feet taking her teensy self down the aisle in satin slippers?

Some days it's hard to be Christian.

Harriet

John

October, 1838

Dear John,

Not a word from you. Have you run away, then? If you
not a Slave anymore, John, dont forget the Slaves you left
behind!

The past month we been lashed by three hard storms
in a row. Each time the clouds hang heavy and dark, and
like a monster, the hurricane springs right at us from the
sea.

I wait out the night rains in the storeroom, but have to
stay in my hole for the day gales. For hours, wild winds
drove rain in through the chinks, leaving me cold and
drenched and feeling punished for something I didn't do.
The water from the rivers is still high in the swamps. And
Gran's patch a mess—all the corn blew over or broke off.

We hear that Samuel and his bride is stopping in New
York, then coming on home. John, please be with them.
So many folks has gone and left me. Will I be talking to
you in my letter Book, too?

Your Harriet

* * *

Dear John,

Gran is weak with sorrow.

The day you all due in Edenton, she makes a big meal and asks some of your friends over. I hear her snap out a clean white apron, tie it on, and announce, My favorite boy going to have his favorite food! She fix black-eyed peas, green beans with fatback, and sweet potato pie. She even laid your plate in its old spot on the table.

Up in my hole, I listen for your step and your voice. When the stagecoach come by, Mark run to the tavern to meet you. But he come home alone, and I hear Gran cry, Where is my grandchild?

Then Samuel sends a boy with a note: John did not return with me and Mrs Sawyer, it read. The abolitionists in New York tricked him into running away.

Poor Samuel. Sometimes I feel sorry for him. He truly believes, Brother, that you too loyal to leave your master unless you been duped.

Must be some kind of White folks' conjer. When it comes to Slavery, they make themselves be blind. And he just cant see: You would be his friend, but you wont be his Slave!

Gran been weeping for hours, though I only hear sniffling now. And a new worry is needled its way into my thoughts. What if Samuel so vexed with you that he sells my children to make up the loss? I know we wish for freedom when we were young. But now that you grab your chance, feels like you left us swinging in the wind.

Aunt Betty say there is sorrow in the Norcom house,

too. Young Benjamin Rush Norcom been wasting away for months and finally is died. Betty says she feels more alone than ever. She raise those Norcom children like they her own, I guess because they all she got.

Harriet

* * *

November, 1838

Dear John,

Last Sunday we been set strate bout what you done. Gran sitting on the piazza with the children—sometimes on a Sabbath she brings them out to play where I can hear them. And I am so proud of them! Louisa turn five last month, and Joseph getting tall as sage grass.

Grandma, he says, is Uncle John gone for good?

Well, Gran just finish up a crying fit over you, John. I hear her chair scrape and all she says is, Hmm.

Grandma, Joseph asks, can Uncle John find our Mama?

And Gran answers, Humph, like she is disgusted with you for running away, and me for giving her white hair, and Joseph for asking so many questions.

Then he says, Why dont you and Uncle Mark and all of us go live with Uncle John and Mama?

Boy, Gran says with a big sigh, you got more questions than a bullfrog got croaks.

And my heart aches when I hear Louisa ask, But how do we find Mama? I dont remember what she looks like.

Then Aunt Sue Bent walks through the gate with one more question to torment Gran. She looks hard at her friend's red eyes and says, What's wrong, Molly?

And Gran tells her, Wont be nobody left to hand me a

drink when I'm dying. Nobody to lay my old body in the ground. She starts to cry again, and says, My grandboy didn't come back with Mister Sawyer—he staid at the North.

I hear old Aunt Sue clap her hands for joy. Is that all you crying for? she says, and laughs. Get down on your knees and bless the Lord. Except for Sarah, my poor children been sold away, she reminds Gran, and I never expect to know where they are. But you know where John is, she says. He's in the free parts, and that's the right place!

She shamed me and Gran both. Wherever you are, little Brother, I hope freedom is shining its big eyes on you.

Your loving sister,
Harriet

*   *   *

29 August, 1839

Dear John,

Gran almost settled down bout you running away. But since we got your letter from New Bedford, Massachusetts, she is all churn up again. I read it to her through the hole in Uncle Mark's wall. John, we all proud that you been working during the day and going to school at night. That makes you the only one of us had any schooling.

But when I get to the part bout you shipping out to sea, Gran bows her head like she in church. She remembers Uncle Stephen's stories bout whaling ships. Scary talk bout harpoonists getting dragged down by the whale and ships breaking up on the rocks. Did you have to tell her you be gone for three years?

Well, I can hear you sassing me back. Yes, so you say,

there's lots of escaped coloured men go out to sea. Yes, and colour dont matter so much if a man can pull an oar and furl a sail. And yes, John, I know you going to have time to practice your reading and writting. But seems like after three years and all that danger, your share of whale oil ought to come to more than 300 dollers. Sounds like another kind of Slavery to me.

Well, anyway, you gone, along with another year of my life.

Harriet

*　*　*

5 January, 1840

Dear John,

A new baby in the Sawyer family. Samuel's little girl, Laura, was baptized at St. Paul's today. Lavinia Sawyer still dont know Samuel already got two children. Mix-up children, some folks call coloured babies with a White Daddy, but they his all the same.

Aunt Betty hears Maria Norcom talking to the Docter in the parlor: I have every intention of informing Mrs Sawyer who is the father of Harriet's children, she tells him. Harriet is an artful devil, she says, and has made a great deal of trouble in our family. Then Norcom walks out, stiff as a rod, and with out a word to his wife. Aunt Betty says he never mentions my name.

Missus blames me that you run away. She is sure I been in the North because of the letters I sent. So she thinks I saw you in New York and talked you into escape.

Well, I dont give two shucks what Maria Norcom thinks. But if Lavinia Sawyer hears about Joseph and Louisa, she might get rid of them. John, John, why cant you be here to help us? All these years of hiding, only to see my girl and boy taken away!

Harriet

*   *   *

25 January, 1840

Dear John,

Gran up most of the night, making cakes and dozens of Snowballs for Norcom's daughter-in-law. You remember it is a tedious receipt that takes much time. When you were a boy you hated paring and stuffing the apples with marmalade before Gran wrap them in pastry. Always hide behind the shed when she call for help. Funny how you were always close by when they come out of the oven.

Well, Gran needed her John last night. Says she could hardly keep her eyes open to make the crackers. But ever since Samuel got married, she been nervous bout the children. She been cooking as much as she can to save for their freedom. Keeps every spare cent in a little bag.

Joseph was sent to buy more cinnamon today and come home mad. He run in the kitchen door saying, Gran, I saw a stranger-lady with Mr Sawyer. She call me a name— says I am a pretty little negro! And she want to know who I belong to.

Well, we know who that stranger lady is. John, I am worn down with worrying bout my babies. Do you remember the old tale Gran used to tell us bout flying back to Affrica? I want to get inside that story. Lift a child under each arm, grab a magic hoe, and sail strate out over the sea.

Harriet

96

*   *   *

26 January, 1840

Dear John,

Lavinia, she knows bout the children and got big plans for them. Her sister from Chicago is visiting. She is taken a liking to Louisa and wants to adopt her. And Lavinia plans to move Joseph to her own house. Poor Gran is all tired out, but she going over to reason with Samuel tonight.

Harriet

*   *   *

27 January, 1840

Dear John,

Samuel thinks the children are not safe here. Says Norcom been bragging that he was tricked into selling them and that they still in his power. So my babies trapped between two masters, like rabbits cornered by hound dogs.

Gran is fixed it so that Samuel and Lavinia will first take Louisa with them to Washington City. I dont like it much. Lavinia might make my daughter maid to her freeborn little sister. I dont want her used that way, even for a short while.

Then they sending her to live with his cousin in Brooklyn, New York. I can join her there if ever I get free. One good thing is she be going to school. How do they treat coloured children in New York? I wish you were here to tell me!

I will say it to you before anybody else. Because Gran and Mark going to raise torment. But I dont care how

97

dangerous it is, my girl going to see her Mama before she
leaves.

Harriet

*   *   *

31 January, 1840
Dear John,

Words, they only poor silent beggars that cant tell how I
feel. Only a Slave Mama could understand.

Mark keep watch at the gate while I slip down to the
piazza and up the steps to my old room. When he lead
my girl in by the hand, she dont know me till I say, Louisa,
I am your Mama. And in a moment, we holding each
other close. Been five long years since I felt the softness
of her cheek.

You really my Mama? she says. But why dont you come
before? There being no easy answer to that question, I
answer it with another.

Do you like to go away? I ask, and she starts to cry.

I dont know, she says. Gran tells me I be going to a
good place where I can learn to read and write. And by
and by I can write her a letter. But I wont have Joseph,
she says, or Gran, or Uncle Mark, or nobody to love me.

And then I make promises that might be false as spring
snow. I will come soon, I tell my Lulu, and bring Joseph
with me. And the three of us going to live together in our
own home and have happy times.

Uncle Mark tells her, Louisa, this is the secret you
promise your grandmama never to tell. If you speak of
this night, you wont ever see your Gran again, and your
Mama cant come to Brooklyn.

I wont never tell, she promises. She is only seven, and Mark looks worried. But I know my daughter. She will not tell.

Louisa fell asleep in my arms. I watch her face all through the moonshiny night. By dawn I was back in my den. And in two hours, I hear her say good-bye to neighbors and friends. The gate slammed, the stagecoach blew its horn, and my child was gone from sight.

Harriet

* * *

March, 1840

Dear John,

I don't know if your niece is dead, dying, or sold and marched down to the Mississippi bottoms. Three months gone by, and not a word from Samuel. I write in Gran's name to Brooklyn, but they say Louisa not there. I write to Washington City, but they dont answer.

John, you were smart to leave Samuel when you did. I been trusting him since the first day I ever climbed into his bed. When he said to you, John, I will free you in five years, I think he ment it. When he says to me, Harriet, I will set your children free, he wants to do it. Samuel Sawyer is not a bad man on purpose. But even a gentleman dont think he has to keep his word to a Slave.

Harriet

* * *

99

June, 1840

Dear John,

Samuel's young cousin is written at last to Gran from Brooklyn. Louisa just got there, and she sends a hidden message in the letter for me: I try to do what you told me, she says, and I pray for you every night.

But the cousin wrote something else that has set me shaking. Mister Sawyer, she writes, has given Louisa to me to be my little waiting maid. I shall send her to school, and I hope someday she will write to you herself.

I dont know what this means! Is Louisa staying there till I can come, or is Samuel given his daughter away as property, only to be sold again in the South?

John, seems like all these years I been a foolish puppy, chasing myself in circles to save the children. I run and run, but I never do catch up.

Harriet

*   *   *

June, 1841

Dear John,

I worry some bout Joseph. For months he dont seem easy in his mind. He does his chores with out a word. Sweeps the yard and totes water from the well for Gran, but the minute he sees a constable or patrol, he runs inside to tell her.

And he misses his sister. Gran says he is been spending many hours fishing in the creek. Or sometimes he goes down to the wharf, like we used to, and skips rocks out into the water. Except he goes alone.

His loneliness hurts me, but I use the time when he is gone to stretch my legs in the storeroom. Mary Matilda Norcom been getting schooling in Philadelphia, and Norcom left last week to visit her. I still send letters to him. Had the last one mailed from Canada. Because of the letters, I believe he is given up on me. But I still rest easier when he is out of town.

Aunt Betty come to visit last night. We talk through the hole in the wall, and she says the Docter sent a box of presents to his children from Norfolk. Red-striped gingham dress cloth for little Elizabeth, a Farmer's Almanack for James, and a Book of letters and pictures for baby William.

Aunt Betty and I whisper-laugh. James got to pay his father for the Almanack, she says, and poor William got to learn to spell in exchange for the Book. And no present at all for Maria, his own wife!

He's too mean to die, I tell Betty. Because the Lord wont want him and the devil wont let him in.

Harriet

*   *   *

2 January, 1842

Dear John,

No morning visit to the storeroom. Got to stick close by my den. The Slave-catchers been sniffing round all day, looking for Aunt Sue Bent's daughter, Sarah. Sarah and her four little girls been split up and sold at the Hiring-Out. Sarah run away.

Patrols come with a big noise early this morning, a-raring and a-tearing through Aunt Sue's little house right

here on the back of Gran's lot. I lay still all the while, hardly moving or breathing, till I hear them leave.

Then Joseph runs to Gran to say he got a glimpse of Sarah in her Mama's hut. Gran told him it was a deep secret and made him swear on the Bible never to tell. Sarah, she got lots of spunk, but I know she is terrified out in that hut. I wish she could share my nook, but it would only put more worry on Gran's back.

Ever since Louisa left, I been thinking my time is bout spent here. And now Samuel says he going to send Joseph North as soon as Uncle Mark can take him. Besides, the shingles are wearing out, and I get soaked with every rain. Mark cant fix the roof with out people seeing me.

Mark and Gran been telling our trusty friends to look for me an escape. Be patient, Mark says, but some days I think I wont last another minute.

Harriet

*   *   *

8 February, 1842

Dear John,

I read through my letter Books and remember all who is left me behind. Parents, uncles, sweetheart. They only shadows to me now, like when nighttime crowds the trees and pushes them out of sight.

But to lose Aunt Betty! This is the hardest of all. Our dear Aunt is struck by paralysis and may be in her death sickness. Gran with her at the Docter's house now. Norcom is treating Betty, but he tells Gran, Where a recovery does not follow the attack in a short time, it very seldom takes place at all.

Mark just come back to say that Betty, she is having trouble talking. But Gran kneels by the bed and holds her daughter's hand. They smiling and talking with their eyes.

Harriet

*   *   *

10 February, 1842

Dear John,

Some sorrow too heavy to hold. Mark come from Norcom's and I hear Aunt Sue downstairs ask, How is she?

She is dead, Mark says. And up in my cell, I faint away. When I opened my eyes, the roof was whirling over my head, and Mark was there. Harriet, he whispers, she died happy.

Toward the end, Aunt Betty held up her hand to let Gran know all was well. Mark says even the Docter cried some. She has always been a faithful servant, he tells Gran, and we shall never be able to replace her. Then they let six-year-old William Norcom come in. Of all the Norcom children Aunt Betty raise, she favor him the most.

I think she been slowly murdered by hard work, John. All my troubles help finish it up. She been the comfort of my life.

No one prised freedom more than our good Aunt. She used to kneel by the hole and whisper to me: I am old and dont have long to live. I could die happy, if only I could see you and the children free. Well, I hope she is found her own Promised Land.

Harriet

*   *   *

Dear John,

I know Aunt Betty is happy being laid away on a Sabbath. Maria Norcom wanted her buried in the White folks' burying ground so her Slave would lie at her feet when the Missus die. But Gran says a flat no! I want Betty to lie with all the rest of my family, she says, and where my own old body will be buried.

So Maria had to comfort her self with the Docter's carriage leading off the procession and her own White preacher saying the service. After years of work and broken rest, seems like the Missus a little late in her affection for our Aunt. But I guess it makes a good show for the Slave-holder to miss her old worn-out servant.

Mark says there were lots of coloured folks, both Slave and free, and a few White people that always been friendly to our family. He say Mrs Norcom did drop a tear or two at the grave. I wonder what Maria Norcom do if she turn and see me standing next to her? Her tears would dry faster than spit on an iron.

I hear poor Gran downstairs now. She is lost her last daughter. God help me, says she, I only got one child left.

Harriet

Aunt Betty

1 June, 1842

Dear Aunt Betty,

A word from you always keep me strong. Nearly seven years is passed over my head since that black night when I climb out the window at Auburn. When Gran and John want me to turn myself in, it was you who sent the message, Dont give up! Now I need a wise head more than ever, but who do I ask?

Peter is just come to see me, grinning like a man in the moon. And he brung some bright shining news. Your day is here, Harriet, he whispers at the trapdoor. I found a chance for you to go to the Free States. You got two weeks to decide.

You would think leaving my cell would be easy as taking a drink of water. But will Joseph be safe? What if Norcom decides my Son still belongs to him? And Gran, she will raise scratch and say she cant stand to lose anymore family.

Time. It creeps and pokes along like a mule all these years. Then suddenly, two weeks dont seem long enough to balance the gladness of freedom against the danger of escape.

Harriet

*   *   *

10 June, 1842

Dear Aunt Betty,

I been thinking it over. I will talk to Joseph before I go, and explain that I be waiting for him at the North. Gran been nocking on the trapdoor every night, crying over missing you and crying over losing me. Last night she says, Write the Docter when you get there. Tell him I will buy you from him.

But I wont have Gran sell her home and everything in it for my free papers. Besides, I remember long years ago and my Daddy saying, In the eyes of God, Harriet, you already free.

Harriet

*   *   *

14 June, 1842

Dear Aunt Betty,

I am to leave by ship tomorrow night. But Gran is carrying on something awful. Charity's Son, James, been caught after running away. They give him a heavy lashing and put him in jail with bread and water.

Rumors flying round town like bees. Folks say they going to put him in the cotton gin and screw it down so he cant move. Gran is scared pink and begging me not to go. Harriet, she moans, you going off smiling, but you be coming back crying. Gran and I, we both remember Uncle Joseph lying in prisan, looking white and spongy as a ghost. And you, Aunt Betty, locked in the cold jail with John and the children.

Now even Uncle Mark telling me to hold off. This fear is a fever spreading through the house. Escape was so simple for John!

Harriet

*   *   *

15 June, 1842

Dear Aunt Betty,

Bad weather coming up, and the ship still sitting out in the Sound. Gran and Mark and I agree. With out involving my name, Gran has give my place to Aunt Sue's Sarah.

The price of taking a stowaway is dear. Same as a ticket to England. But a chance for freedom dont come round too often. We cant fling it away, not when Sarah needs help. Peter is disappointed with me. But he fix it so Sarah can board the ship tonight.

Harriet

*   *   *

17 June, 1842

Dear Aunt Betty,

The weather been stormy for two days now, and the ship is still not left. Peter told us poor Sarah was scared nigh to death when they carry her out to her cabin. And with high waves tossing the boat, this waiting must be a torment to her.

107

Gran thinks Sarah will be caught and we will all hang between the heavens and earth til we dead, dead, dead. Aunt Betty, your mother is aged since you left us. Her face is lined with the worries of seventy-three years. I try to calm her, but we been together so long. What she feels, I feel. So we both half-crazy with fear.

Harriet

*   *   *

18 June, 1842

Dear Aunt Betty,

I write to you with trembling hands. This morning Gran raps her signal for me to come down to the storeroom. We are looking out at the clearing skies and talking bout the ship. Then we hear that sneaky Jenny out on the piazza.

I been hunting everywhere for you, Aunt Molly, she calls, all sugar-sweet. Missus Blount wants you to send her some crackers.

Silently I slip down behind a barrel, but my heart beat loud as the wings of a wild turkey. Gran quick shuts the storeroom door, locks it, and goes with Jenny to count the crackers.

A few minutes later Gran come back. Poor child! she says, my carelessness is ruined you. The boat ain't gone yet. Get ready right now, and go with Sarah. I ain't got another word to say against it now, for there's no telling what may happen this day.

So here I sit, back in my hole, waiting for Peter to see if the captain will take another runaway. And who knows where Jenny is flapping her jaws? If she did see me, she knows better than to admit to Martha Blount that she been nosing round. And the Norcoms wont agree to talk to some gossipy Slave till after supper.

But I know that household too well. They done eating by dusk—just at the time I will walk to the wharf.

Harriet

*   *   *

Afternoon

Dear Aunt Betty,

Less than an hour before leaving here forever. Peter be waiting for me in the street soon. Gran brung Joseph to me in the storeroom. My poor boy hardly knows what to think. Seeing his Mama appear for the first time in seven years, only to hear she leaving again.

But you know my Son, Aunt Betty. You watched over him, same as you watched over me and John when we lived in the Norcom house. He is wiser than his twelve years. Joseph says, Mama, I been so afraid they coming to catch you!

How did you find out? I ask him, surprised.

I was standing under the eaves one day, he says, and I hear somebody cough up over the storeroom. I dont know what made me think it was you, but I did.

And this is why he been so watchful, always running to Gran if he smells danger nearby. I hear him many a time playing with other children and talking bout me being in the North.

Joseph, I promise him, one day the Lord going to send you to me, and we will live together with Louisa.

Then he starts to tell me how Gran is not passed a bite

of food by her lips all day. When in come Gran with her bag of money. I beg her to keep it to pay for Joseph's way North.

But you might get sick among strangers, she says, and they would send you to the poorhouse to die! Oh, my good grandmother.

I look round at these rough walls. They been hateful as poison, but they done the job. And now I stop this letter. Gran calling me to climb down and pray. Dear Aunt Betty, I know you are next to the Lord. You pray, too.

Harriet

*　*　*

Evening

Dear Aunt Betty,

Worry sticking to me like cockleburs. The captain, he has our ticket money now. Nothing to stop him from turning us in for the reward. But Sarah says dont fret. In her three days on the ship everybody been kind.

When the captain brung me down to our little box of a cabin, Sarah just sat there with her mouth open. Harriet, is it you, she says, or your ghost? We hold each other tight, and my fears flow out in great sobs.

Then the captain comes back to shush us. For my safety and yours, he says, it would be prudent not to attract any attention. As far as the sailors know, he told us, you are Women going to meet your husbands in Philadelphia.

The boat is passing the Snaky Swamp now, and there is still enough light to make out the buildings that rim the bay. From here, Edenton is a toy town, like the ones John used to make out of sticks and sand. The wind is against us, so the boat moves slow as a giant snail. Me and Sarah, we anxious to put the miles behind us. Dont want to be playing peep squirrel with the constables who search the ships.

I am weary in my bones, but I wont sleep. Not when I can still feel Joseph pulling at my arm down by the wharf. I been looking in the Docter's window, he tells me as I climb in the rowboat, and he's at home. Good-bye, Mama, Joseph says, and waves. Dont cry, I'll come! Then my fine boy turns and runs back home.

Well, I am breaking that promise bout crying.

Harriet

* * *

19 June, 1842

Dear Aunt Betty,

This I will remember till the longest day I live: the sunshine warming my skin, the breeze sliding by my cheeks. Dear old friend, we are sailing along the Chesapeake Bay like butterflies on the sky!

The captain says ten days till we land in Philadelphia. I still got suspicions, but I try to swallow them. Captain says he was born and raised in the Slave States and his Brother was a Slave-trader. I guess he's trying to make up for evil done by his kin. But it's hard to trust a White man.

He says we can stay above board all day, unless a sail hoves in sight. I walk up and down the deck till my wobbly legs give way. And Sarah and I been talking like starving folks eat.

She rubs my poor limbs with saltwater while I tell her

the story of my hiding years. Then I hold her hands while she tells me bout losing her girls on that awful auction day. Sarah is suffered more than me, because her babies gone forever.

I spare her my thoughts bout Louisa. But I cant help smiling inside. My arms be wrapped round my Lulu in only a few weeks, if the captain dont sell us and the boat dont sink.

Harriet

*   *   *

Molly Horniblow
King Street
Edenton, N.C.
30 June, 1842

Dear Gran,

This is the first real letter I ever sent to my family. Be strange to tear the page from my Book and know it will be delivered. The captain will make sure you get it, but mind who reads it to you. Make sure they trusty.

Sarah and I looking for the sun to come up. I wont let on where we are, but a big city waits for us right outside this ship. Go on shore in broad daylight, the captain says, as the best way to avoid confusion.

Gran, you wouldn't know your Harriet. Moving round and rubbing with saltwater is helped my legs. I can almost walk regular. But my face! It's blistered from the sun and wind. I am peeling like the bark of a birch tree.

First thing Sarah and I going to find is a shop that sells double veils and gloves. That way we can look out at people, but they cant stare so easy at us. Next thing is to find some folks to help us. You know they always saying the poor Slave got many friends in the North. Well, we fixing to see if that is true.

Then I got to find a way to New York and Louisa. Hope those bluebloods been good to her. I wonder, can she read and write? In all her nine years, she was only with her Mama in her baby time. I cant give the years back and am troubled in my heart bout it.

I will write to you when we settled in New York, so Mark can bring Joseph. My Son had to grow up too fast. Hope I can put the light back in his serious eyes.

When I get my children, I will go look for John up in New Bedford. And if the Lord can spare me any more happiness, our John be back from his voyage in one piece. Then we can be a family together, maybe in a little house all our own. And you'll be with me, too, dear grandmother—I be feeling your arm round my shoulder wherever I go.

The waves all sparkly with light now, Gran, and the city is stretch out in front of us. For the first time ever in my life, I see the sun rising on freedom.

Your loving Harriet

PART III
1842–1897

Harriet:
The Rest of Her Story

1842–1852

When Harriet Ann Jacobs stepped from the rowboat onto the wharf in Philadelphia, she saw a world quite different from the gray, sandy streets of Edenton. It was a "city of strangers," she later remembered, "an unknown tide of life." The cobbled avenues were swollen with people, the air filled with cries of hawkers selling fresh fish, fruit, and vegetables.

Within minutes the captain introduced her to a black minister, whose family welcomed and sheltered her for the next five days. Riding in a crowded segregated train car, Harriet then traveled to New York, where she found Louisa living with Samuel Sawyer's cousins.

She was on free soil, but she was still not free from problems. The cousins had not sent Louisa to school, and planned instead to make her a waiting-maid. Harriet was not completely recovered from her seven years in the garret—if she walked too much, her legs became swollen. And she needed a job and a place to live.

She soon found work as nursemaid for a new baby in the family of Nathaniel Parker Willis. Mrs. Willis was a kind employer, calling for the doctor when Harriet's legs swelled and encouraging her to bring Louisa to live with them. But Samuel Sawyer still controlled his daughter's fate, and Harriet didn't want to risk angering his cousins by taking Louisa.

It was a healing, but frustrating, time for her. Although she lived in a free state, she was not allowed to sit with white people in public places such as streetcars and restaurants. She was fond of the Willises' little girl, but her own daughter was only a few miles away, neglected and lonely. Grateful for lodging in the Astor Hotel with the Willis family, she still longed for a home of her own. "Sweet and bitter," she said, "were mixed in the cup of my life. . . ."

Within six months, she enjoyed two partial reunions with her family. John S. Jacobs returned from his whaling voyage in February of 1843, located Harriet and Louisa in New York, and stayed a week before moving to Boston. Later that year, Harriet heard that Dr. Norcom was coming to New York. Afraid for her safety, she quickly made plans to join John in Boston, and got word to Gran to send Joseph there by ship.

By 1844, and after another attempt by the Norcom family to find her, Harriet was finally able to bring Louisa to Boston. Not since her first escape from Auburn plantation nine years earlier had she been able to embrace both of her children at once. And for a brief time, the dream of living with her little family under one roof came true. "The winter passed pleasantly," she remembered of 1844–1845, "while I was busy with my needle, and my children with their books."

118

After Mrs. Willis died in childbirth, Mr. Willis offered Harriet a job as nursemaid for the baby on a family trip to England. To earn money, Harriet agreed, leaving the children in Boston. Louisa went to school, and fifteen-year-old Joseph was apprenticed to a printer. But by the time she returned, her son, shunned by his white fellow-apprentices and miserable, had shipped out to sea on a whaling voyage.

Until 1849, Harriet and Louisa continued to live in Boston on Charter Street in two "homelike" little rooms. Her dressmaking skills provided a comfortable income, and although she didn't own her home, Harriet must have felt contented during these years. At last she was able to give her daughter the same warm, protecting environment they had both found in Gran's cozy house.

When John offered to send Louisa to a school for young black students in upstate New York, Harriet reluctantly agreed. "It seemed as if all the sunshine had gone away," she recalled. "My little room was dreadfully lonely." The pain of separation eased a little when John suggested that they both move to Rochester, New York. Harriet would be closer to Louisa's school, and they could open an antislavery reading room.

It would also put her farther from the reach of the Norcom family. Little Mary Matilda Norcom had grown into a grasping, foolish young woman. In 1846 she married a ne'er-do-well aptly named Daniel Messmore, and the family's shocked reactions led to violence between Messmore and the Norcom sons. The doctor never forgave his daughter, and the Messmores moved away.

By the time Harriet moved to Rochester in March of 1849, the Norcom family had already harassed her with letters meant to cajole and trick her into returning to

Edenton. Eventually, as legal slave trade decreased and Harriet's value as a slave increased, the Messmores would do far more than write letters to put money in their empty pockets.

Harriet's year in Rochester expanded her world. She now knew Frederick Douglass on a first-name basis, and her circle of friends included many abolitionists. But the Jacobses' reading room, located above the offices of Douglass's newspaper, was not a financial success. Nor was John's Oyster Saloon. After Joseph returned from sea in May of 1849, he and John left to find their fortunes in the gold fields of California.

"I was alone again," Harriet remembered, and once more, she needed to find work. She returned to New York in September of 1850 and was again employed by the Willis family—the new Mrs. Willis had a two-year-old son and a baby girl. Cornelia Willis hated slavery and proved to be Harriet's greatest defense against the most dangerous weapon she would face since her escape: the Fugitive Slave Law of 1850.

Harriet spent an anxious winter in New York, knowing that because she had escaped from a state where slavery was legal, she could be captured by slave-hunters and sent back to the Norcoms. Now Harriet traveled only the back streets of the city, keeping her head low, but looking closely at every face. Anyone could be a kidnapper. Anyone could steal her away to slavery. "I never go out in the daylight," she wrote to a friend in Rochester, "accept I ride insite."

Harriet learned in a letter from Gran that Dr. Norcom had died in November 1850. A later letter warned her that Maria Norcom still considered Harriet her daughter's property. Apparently Mary Matilda agreed.

Harriet became more cautious than ever. When she read the daily newspaper, she always checked the column called "Arrivals at City Hotels." In March of 1852 she was horrified to see Daniel Messmore's name listed. She fled immediately to another part of the city, and within hours, the Messmores were at the Willis doorstep, claiming that Harriet and her children still belonged to Mary Matilda.

In the midst of a heavy snowstorm, Harriet was sent to New Bedford, Massachusetts, by Mrs. Willis, who urged her to take the baby with her so that no one would suspect she was a fugitive slave. While in New Bedford, Harriet, "weary of flying from pillar to post," decided to join John in California.

But the chase was already over. Mrs. Willis arranged to pay the Messmores three hundred dollars to forever give up all claims on Harriet and her children. "I am rejoiced to tell you," Mrs. Willis wrote Harriet, "that the money for your freedom has been paid. . . . Come home tomorrow. I long to see you and my sweet babe."

Harriet was both relieved and appalled. The words *Bill of Sale* struck her like a blow. "So I was *sold* at last!" she wrote. "A human being *sold* in the free city of New York!" But now the rest of the world would recognize what she had always known: Harriet Ann Jacobs was free.

1853–1870

These were painful but productive years for Harriet. Molly Horniblow, eighty-three and so feeble that she could no longer attend church, lived long enough to hear the good news of Harriet's freedom. But she never saw her granddaughter again. In late summer of 1853 a letter with a black seal arrived in New York, telling Harriet that Gran had died. Funeral services were held at St. Paul's Episcopal Church on September 4. "She had gone," Harriet paraphrased from the Bible, "where the wicked cease from troubling, and the weary are at rest."

Five years later, Harriet would receive Uncle Mark's obituary in the mail. "They call him a good man and a useful citizen," the notice read. Mark, who married the year after Harriet's escape, had supported himself as a barber, running a shop in one of the outbuildings on Gran's lot. With his death, Harriet's Edenton family was gone.

Although John S. Jacobs was safe from the Fugitive Slave Law because he had run away while living in a free state, he was so disgusted with the law that he left the country. The gold-mining venture had been unsuccessful, and he moved to Australia in 1857, taking Joseph with him. Except for one letter, it would be the last time Harriet would see or hear from her son.

By 1858, John had moved to England, where he married an Englishwoman and published his autobiography in a magazine. He returned to New York only after the Civil War began. By 1857, Louisa had finished her studies and was employed as a governess on Long Island. She managed to visit Harriet occasionally at the Willises' country estate on the Hudson River.

Harriet remained with the Willis family until the Civil War started in 1861. During these years, urged by Amy Post, an abolitionist from Rochester, she secretly began to write about her experiences. She started with an anonymous letter in 1853 to a New York newspaper, telling the story of her life in an article headed LETTER FROM A FUGITIVE SLAVE. This was followed by more letters, all unsigned. She did not tell her employers about her work—partly out of embarrassment over her lack of education, partly because she thought Nathaniel Willis was proslavery.

Then Harriet began a book that would tell her whole story. She wrote alone in her room at night, sometimes bedridden with severe attacks of rheumatism, and often too busy with household duties to work on her own project. ". . . if I could steal away and have two quiet Months to myself," she wrote to Amy Post, "I would work night and day though it should all fall to the ground—to get this time I should have to explain myself and no one here except Louisa knows that I have even written anything to be put in print."

Harriet had resolved to tell the story of slavery from a woman's point of view, although it meant revealing "so many painful things in it that makes me shrink," including the sexual nature of her relationship with Samuel Sawyer. In 1858, Harriet finished her book, *Linda: Incidents in the Life of a Slave Girl, Written by Herself*. After a string of difficulties with publishers, she brought the book out herself in January 1861, under the pseudonym Linda Brent. Three months later, the Civil War began.

Only forty-eight years old, Harriet had experienced a lifetime of suffering. And with her book, she had made a unique contribution to the antislavery cause. *Incidents* revealed the sexual aspects of slavery, which were thought to be too vulgar for delicate ears. As the *Weekly Anglo-African* newspaper said on April 18, 1861, "It is the 'oft-told tale' of American slavery, in another and more revolting phase than that which is generally seen." By telling her story, Harriet brought sexual abuse by slaveholders into the public eye and broke the silence for all enslaved black women.

But her work was not done. She was still Daniel Jacobs's

determined daughter. During and after the war she and Louisa, who was trained to be a schoolteacher, did relief work for black refugees who ran for safety behind Union lines in Washington, D.C., and Alexandria, Virginia. The freed men and women were starved for learning. One Union soldier wrote to his family that everywhere he went in Alexandria, he saw blacks with books and paper, teaching themselves to read and spell.

No longer shy about writing and signing her letters, Harriet campaigned for help for her people. In April of 1863, she wrote from Alexandria to Boston for aid:

> We have 125 scholars; we have no paid teachers as yet, the children have been taught by convalescent soldiers, who kindly volunteer their services until called to join their regiment. We need female teachers: the little ones are apt . . . I have a large sewing class of children and adults.

She even made trips back to Boston with orphaned children, appearing with them at antislavery meetings with the hope of finding homes for them. She was always successful. Like her grandmother, Harriet soothed and comforted those who needed her.

After the war, Harriet and Louisa put their own needs aside and continued to volunteer their services. They spent two years in Savannah, Georgia, helping dispense food and clothing and starting schools, nursing homes, and orphanages. Harriet stopped in Edenton in 1867 on one of her trips south, and wrote to a friend:

> I felt I would like to write you a line from my old home. I am sitting under the old roof twelve feet from

the spot where I suffered all the crushing weight of slavery. . . . I cannot tell you how I feel in this place, the change is so great I can hardly take it in. . . . I have hunted up all the old people, done what I could for them. I love to work for these old people. [M]any of them I have known from Childhood. . . . [M]y love to Miss Daisy. I send her some Jassmine blossoms. . . . [T]ell her they bear the fragrance of freedom.

1870–1897

By 1870, Harriet was running a boardinghouse in Cambridge, Massachusetts. She also worked as a matron for the Women's Club in nearby Boston. In 1875, her beloved brother died and was buried in Cambridge. Still with Louisa, Harriet moved to Washington, D.C., in 1878, where her daughter was active in the National Association of Colored Women.

In 1892, Harriet sold her grandmother's house for 425 dollars. The little home where she had run to Gran for comfort, where she had given birth, where she had spent seven tortured years as a fugitive, was torn down immediately. A hardware store now sits on the lot. The jail, which remained in use until 1980, still stands. Now called Mount Auburn, the plantation house where Harriet began her quest for freedom has been moved six miles from its original site and restored.

On a Sunday morning in March 1897, Harriet Ann Jacobs died at the age of eighty-three. She ended her journey in Mount Auburn Cemetery, Cambridge, buried next to her brother. The Reverend Francis Grimké, a former slave and a well-known citizen of Washington, D.C., shared his impressions of Harriet in his eulogy. He remembered her "kind, benevolent face," and the "warm grasp of her friendly hand." Harriet Ann Jacobs was a "woman of strong character," he recalled, who "knew how to say, No." But there was in her "a heart as tender as a little child."

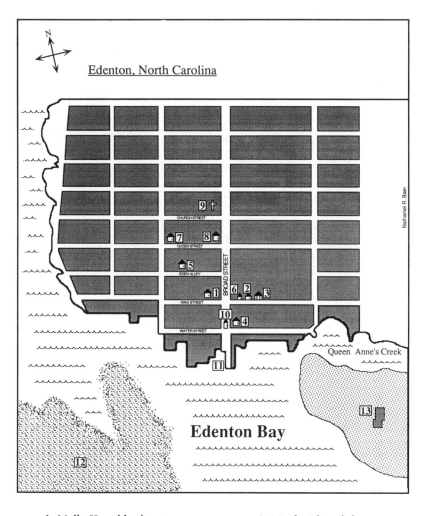

Edenton, North Carolina

1. Molly Horniblow's cottage
2. Horniblow's Tavern
3. Chowan County Courthouse and Jail
4. Josiah Collins's town house
5. Dr. James Norcom's home
6. Dr. Norcom's office
7. Samuel Sawyer's home
8. Martha Blount's home
9. St. Paul's Church
10. Market House
11. Public Wharf
12. Snaky Swamp
13. Hayes Plantation

A map of Edenton, North Carolina, 1813–1842. *Nathaniel R. Baer.*

The Edenton waterfront in 1973. The town house belonging to Josiah Collins, Joseph Horniblow's master, is on the far left. The cupola of the courthouse can be seen behind it. *North Carolina State Archives.*

Dr. James Norcom's house on Eden Alley shortly before it was torn down in 1957. *Collection of the Museum of Early Southern Decorative Arts, Winston-Salem, North Carolina.*

Left, a photograph of a daguerreotype presumed to be a likeness of Dr. James Norcom, Sr., in 1847 at the age of sixty-nine; *right*, Maria Norcom. *North Carolina State Archives.*

The back of the Chowan County jail. After the Nat Turner revolt in 1831, at least twenty-one blacks were jailed on suspicion of rebellion. *North Carolina State Archives.*

Above, the parlor and, *below*, the bedchamber of Dr. James Norcom's house on Eden Alley. The late eighteenth-century furnish-
ings are similar to those that the Norcoms would have used.
*Collection of the Museum of Early Southern Decorative Arts,
Winston-Salem, North Carolina.*

INCIDENTS

IN THE

LIFE OF A SLAVE GIRL.

WRITTEN BY HERSELF.

"Northerners know nothing at all about Slavery. They think it is perpetual bondage only. They have no conception of the depth of *degradation* involved in that word, SLAVERY; if they had, they would never cease their efforts until so horrible a system was overthrown."

A WOMAN OF NORTH CAROLINA.

"Rise up, ye women that are at ease! Hear my voice, ye careless daughters! Give ear unto my speech."

ISAIAH xxxii. 9.

EDITED BY L. MARIA CHILD.

BOSTON:
PUBLISHED FOR THE AUTHOR.
1861.

Title page of Harriet Jacobs's autobiography. *Alderman Library, University of Virginia.*

A drawing of Molly Horniblow's cottage on King Street. Built in the late eighteenth century, it once belonged to a silversmith. *Nancy Takahashi.*

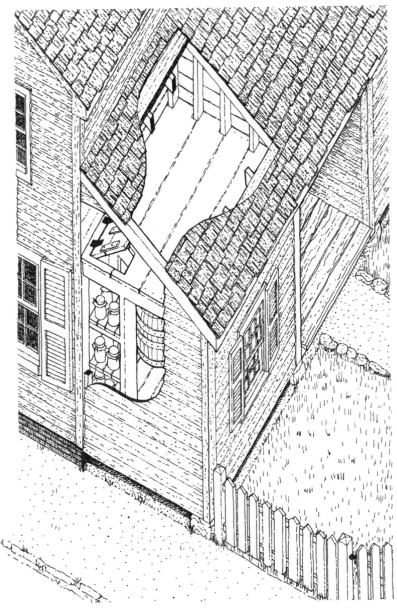

A drawing of the garret where Harriet Jacobs hid for almost seven years. *Nancy Takahashi.*

Auburn Plantation, 1966. Harriet Jacobs escaped from one of the parlor windows opening onto the front porch. *North Carolina State Archives.*

The graves of Harriet Jacobs and Louisa Matilda Jacobs in Mount Auburn Cemetery, Cambridge, Massachusetts. Harriet's headstone is inscribed: "Patient in tribulation, fervent in spirit serving the Lord." *Courtesy of Janet Heywood, Friends of Mount Auburn Cemetery, Cambridge, Massachusetts.*

AUTHOR'S NOTE

Harriet Ann Jacobs did not actually write *Letters from a Slave Girl.* But a biographer is also a storyteller, and after reading Harriet's correspondence, a letter format seemed the natural way to tell her story.

Letters also suit Harriet's biography because learning to read and write was a rare accomplishment for an enslaved child. Many slaveholders were fearful that literate slaves would be more difficult to control. After the Nat Turner rebellion in 1831, laws were passed in North Carolina making it a crime to teach a slave. Almost every North Carolina slave narrative mentions that no books or learning of any kind were allowed. Reimagining Harriet's life in letter form celebrates her determination to become educated even while in bondage.

In Harriet's time, writing paper was handmade, expensive, and hoarded like money. It was common practice to fill every available inch of old account books with reminders, lists, and diary entries. Sometimes the book was turned sideways and the spaces between the lines were filled in with more words!

Her first mistress did teach her to read, but Harriet

taught herself to write. Children in her day learned to write by copying lines of text into a practice book, or copybook. Lacking a proper copybook of her own, it is likely that young Harriet would have written on scrap paper, such as a used account book.

Like *Letters from a Slave Girl*, much of Harriet's actual writing during her years in Edenton, North Carolina, was of a private nature. We know that she had to conceal her literacy from her master. "One day," she recalled in *Incidents in the Life of a Slave Girl*, "he caught me teaching myself to write." We also know that she received notes and poems from friends. Since writing was forbidden, it is likely that she responded to them in secret. A thoughtful person, Harriet may also have kept a journal.

Like the letters herein, young Harriet Ann Jacobs's real writing was probably quite personal. In a world that did not recognize her humanity or her emotions, such writing may have provided the only safe way to express her deepest feelings.

To retell portions of Harriet's story, particularly her childhood years, I reconstructed details that would bring her to life: social occasions, meals eaten, words spoken. (Even Harriet, when recalling events from years long past, had to make up dialogue for her autobiography.) But the major events in *Letters from a Slave Girl* are true. Every person and place mentioned in the letters really existed. Even the weather conditions are accurate.

To protect friends and relatives still living in slavery when she wrote her narrative, Harriet omitted dates and used fictitious names. I kept these false names when real names were not available, or created names when she gave none at all. When necessary, I estimated dates.

When the older Harriet published *Incidents*, she had been living in the North for nineteen years. She felt comfortable writing in the language of her readers, who were educated Northern white women. But the younger Harriet would have spoken and written in the Southern black dialect of her native state—a dialect somewhat diluted by spending eight childhood years with white mistresses. To recreate this voice, I flavored *Letters* with folk expressions inspired by the rich oral language of former North Carolina slaves.

The first half of *Letters from a Slave Girl* contains spelling and grammar patterns harvested from the letters of Harriet's brother, John S. Jacobs. I have also used spelling and grammar patterns from letters actually written by Harriet Jacobs. Like John, she had little or no formal instruction in writing, and often invented ways to spell and use words. "I never studied Grammer," she once wrote to a friend, "therefore I know nothing about it."

Because most slaves were not literate, there is little firsthand information on what life was like for them. To recreate the details of Harriet's life as a slave in Edenton, I relied on the 1987 Harvard University Press edition of her narrative, her brother's narrative, the Norcom family papers, the records of nearby plantations, Edenton newspapers, and books about Edenton during the years that she lived there.

And although there were two million enslaved women, most slave narratives were by black men. To interpret Harriet's life as a black girl, woman, and mother, I used her book, as well as recent books that reconstruct the lives of black and white women of that time. I also drew on information from the oral recollections of former slave women, particularly those from North Carolina.

THE FAMILIES

THE WHITE HORNIBLOW FAMILY

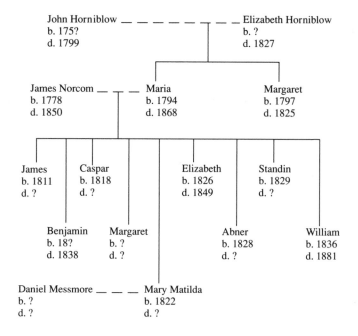

John Horniblow _ _ _ _ _ _ _ _ Elizabeth Horniblow
b. 175?   b. ?
d. 1799   d. 1827

James Norcom _ _ _ Maria   Margaret
b. 1778   b. 1794   b. 1797
d. 1850   d. 1868   d. 1825

James   Caspar   Elizabeth   Standin
b. 1811   b. 1818   b. 1826   b. 1829
d. ?   d. ?   d. 1849   d. ?

Benjamin   Margaret   Abner   William
b. 18?   b. ?   b. 1828   b. 1836
d. 1838   d. ?   d. ?   d. 1881

Daniel Messmore _ _ _ Mary Matilda
b. ?   b. 1822
d. ?   d. ?

THE BLACK HORNIBLOW FAMILY

Sometime between 1780 and 1782, John Horniblow purchased Molly's mother and her three children. As was often the case, they were given the last name of the slaveholder. When John Horniblow died, he left his slaves to his widow, Elizabeth Horniblow.

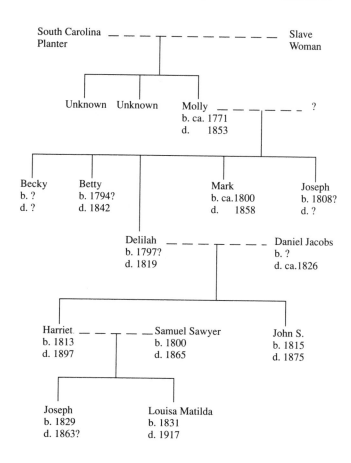

South Carolina Planter _ _ _ _ _ _ _ _ _ _ _ _ Slave Woman

Unknown   Unknown   Molly _ _ _ _ _ _ ?
b. ca. 1771
d.   1853

Becky   Betty   Mark   Joseph
b. ?   b. 1794?   b. ca.1800   b. 1808?
d. ?   d. 1842   d.   1858   d. ?

Delilah _ _ _ _ _ _ _ Daniel Jacobs
b. 1797?   b. ?
d. 1819   d. ca.1826

Harriet _ _ _ _ _ Samuel Sawyer   John S.
b. 1813   b. 1800   b. 1815
d. 1897   d. 1865   d. 1875

Joseph   Louisa Matilda
b. 1829   b. 1831
d. 1863?   d. 1917

NINETEENTH-CENTURY WORDS

BLOODLETTING   A medical practice in both ancient and modern times. Doctors believed that impurities in the blood caused many illnesses and that bleeding would cure the patient. General bloodletting involved making a cut in an artery or vein. For local bloodletting, the doctor made an incision in a smaller vessel and caught the blood in a cup, or applied a leech to suck it out. Some doctors used bleeding as preventative medicine, as witnessed by a former North Carolina slave: "We were bled every year in the spring and fall. He had a little lance. He corded your arm and popped it in and the blood would fly. He took nearly a quart from Grandma—bled us according to size and age."

GUMBO BOX   A box covered with sheepskin that served as a drum for the Johnkannaus dancers. The gumbo box may have African origins. It is similar to a West African drum found on the Gold Coast in the nineteenth century—a hollowed section of tree trunk with sheepskin stretched over one end.

HEROIC MEDICINE   James Norcom, Sr., received his training from Benjamin Rush, a leading medical authority of the late eighteenth century. Rush advocated "heroic" medicine. This included blistering, massive purging of the intestinal tract, and bloodletting. Many slaves were reluctant to submit to these harsh "cures" and chose to treat themselves with home remedies such as teas made from herbs, roots, and bark.

JOHNKANNAUS These dancers and their Christmas celebration are believed to be West African in origin. Also known as *John Kooner* or *John Canoe*, they are an example of how enslaved Africans adapted their culture to the religious practices of their captors. Widely practiced throughout the Caribbean islands, the festival was probably limited on the North American continent to the North Carolina coast. It may have been brought to North Carolina by a shipment of African slaves purchased by Josiah Collins I. He was the owner of Somerset Plantation near Edenton and father of Joseph Horniblow's master, Josiah Collins II. The festival is still celebrated in Jamaica as *Jonkonnu* and in Bermuda as *Gombay*.

JUMPING THE BROOM Marriage between slaves was not legally recognized, but it was encouraged by slaveholders who wanted to discourage runaways and to produce more slaves. Couples were usually married during Christmas week. Since the slaves were already allowed these days off, less work was missed, and there was more time for wedding festivities. Sometimes the master provided a minister to perform the ceremony, but simple broomstick weddings were more common. One former slave from North Carolina remembered that the wedding couple jumped backward over the broomstick. The one who landed on both feet without falling would always have "say-so" over the other.

PATTYROLLERS Also called *patterrollers* or *patrollers*. These small groups of white men policed slave quarters, slave gatherings, and the roads between plantations within their own county. They took turns riding patrol for one, three, or six months at a time.

PECK A poor Southern white, especially a farmer.

PERU-BARK A term for natural quinine, which was made from the bark of the cinchona plant and used to treat the chills and fever of malaria. Malaria was a severe health problem in the coastal areas of the South because malaria-carrying mosquitoes survived the warm winters. Once contracted, the fever would return periodically, or intermittently—thus, the term *mittent* fever.

BIBLIOGRAPHY

Titles marked by an asterisk are most suitable for young readers.

Andrews, William. *To Tell a Free Story: The First Century of Afro-American Autobiography, 1760–1865*. Chicago: University of Illinois Press, 1986.

Barber, James. *Alexandria in the Civil War*. Lynchburg, Va.: H. E. Howard, 1988.

Bassett, John Spencer. *Slavery in the State of North Carolina*. 1899. Reprint. New York: AMS Press, 1972.

The Black Abolitionist Papers, 1830–1865. Sanford, N.C.: Microfilming Corporation of America, 1981. Microfilm reels 12–16.

Braxton, Joanne M. "Harriet Jacobs' *Incidents in the Life of a Slave Girl*: The Redefinition of the Slave Narrative Genre." *Massachusetts Review* 27 (1986): 379–87.

Brodsky, Marc D. *The Courthouse at Edenton*. Edenton, N.C.: Chowan County, 1989.

Carby, Hazel V. *Reconstructing Womanhood: The Emergence of the Afro-American Woman Novelist*. New York: Oxford University Press, 1987.

*Clayton, Thomas H. *Close to the Land: The Way We Lived in North Carolina, 1820–1870*. Chapel Hill: University of North Carolina Press, 1983.

Davis, Charles T., and Henry Louis Gates, Jr. *The Slave's Narrative*. New York: Oxford University Press, 1985.

Farr, James Barker. *Black Odyssey: The Seafaring Traditions of Afro-Americans.* New York: Peter Lang, 1989.

Fenn, Elizabeth A. " 'A Perfect Equality Seemed to Reign': Slave Society and Jonkonnu." *The North Carolina Historical Review* 45 (April 1988): 127–153.

Fox-Genovese, Elizabeth, "My Statue, My Self: Autobiographical Writings of Afro-American Women." In *The Private Self: Theory and Practice of Women's Autobiographical Writings*, edited by Shari Benstock. Chapel Hill: University of North Carolina Press, 1988.

———. *Within the Plantation Household: Black and White Women of the Old South.* Chapel Hill: University of North Carolina Press, 1986.

Genovese, Eugene D. "The Medical and Insurance Costs of Slaveholding in the Cotton Belt." *The Journal of Negro History* 45 (July 1960): 141–155.

———. *Roll, Jordan, Roll: The World the Slaves Made.* New York: Random House, 1976.

Gwin, Minrose C. "Green-Eyed Monsters of the Slavocracy: Jealous Mistresses in Two Slave Narratives." In *Conjuring: Black Women, Fiction, and Literary Tradition*, edited by Marjorie Pryse and Hortense J. Spillers. Bloomington: Indiana University Press, 1986.

*Hughes, Christopher T. "African-American Foodways at Lake Phelps." In *A Taste of the Past: Early Foodways of the Albemarle Region 1585–1830*, edited by Barbara E. Taylor. Elizabeth City, N.C.: Museum of the Albemarle, 1991.

*Hurmence, Belinda, ed. *Before Freedom, When I Can Just Remember: Twenty-Seven Oral Histories of Former South Carolina Slaves.* Winston-Salem, N.C.: J. F. Blair, 1989.

*———. *My Folks Don't Want Me to Talk about Slavery.* Winston-Salem, N.C.: J. F. Blair, 1986.

*Jacobs, Harriet Ann. *Incidents in the Life of a Slave Girl: Written by Herself.* Reprint, with introduction and notes by Jean Fagan Yellin. Cambridge: Harvard University Press, 1987.

———. Letter to Ednah Dow Cheney. Sophia Smith Collection, Smith College, Northampton, Massachusetts.

———. "Letter to J. Sella Martin." *Freeman's Aid Society* 7, 13 April 1863.

————. Letters to Amy Post. Post Papers, University of Rochester, Rochester, New York.

Jacobs, John S. "A True Tale of Slavery." *Leisure Hour* 10 (1861). Chapters 1–7.

"John S. Jacobs to Isaac Post 5 June 1861." In *The Black Abolitionist Papers*. Vol. 1, *The British Isles, 1830–1865*. Edited by C. Peter Ripley. Chapel Hill: University of North Carolina Press, 1983.

Lemmon, Sarah McCulloh, ed. *The Pettigrew Papers*. 2 vols. Raleigh: North Carolina Division of Archives and History, 1988.

"Linda." *The Weekly Anglo-African*, 13 April 1861, sec. 1: 1.

McCully, Helen, ed. *The American Heritage Cookbook and Illustrated History of American Eating & Drinking: Menus and Recipes*. New York: American Heritage Publishing Company, 1964.

MacKethan, Lucinda H. *Daughters of Time: Creating Woman's Voice in Southern Story*. Athens: University of Georgia Press, 1990.

Morris, Charles Edward. "Panic and Reprisal: Reaction in North Carolina to the Nat Turner Insurrection, 1831." *North Carolina Historical Review* 42 (January, 1985): 29–52.

Norcom Family Papers. 1805–1873. North Carolina State Archives.

Parramore, Thomas C. "Harriet Jacobs, James Norcom, and the Defense of Hierarchy." *Carolina Comments* 38 (May 1990): 82–87.

Puckett, Newbell Niles. *Folk Beliefs of the Southern Negro*. Chapel Hill: University of North Carolina Press, 1926.

Rawick, George P. *North Carolina Narratives*. Vols. 14–15 of *The American Slave: A Composite Autobiography*. Westport, CT: Greenwood Publishing Company, 1972.

*Redford, Dorothy Spruill, with Michael D'Orso. *Somerset Homecoming: Recovering a Lost Heritage*. New York: Doubleday, 1988.

Savitt, Todd L. "Slave Health and Southern Distinctiveness." In *Disease and Distinctiveness in the American South*. Edited by Todd L. Savitt and James Harvey Young. Knoxville: University of Tennessee Press, 1988.

Smith, Valerie. *Self-Discovery and Authority in Afro-American Narrative*. Cambridge, MA: Harvard University Press, 1987.

Smyth, William D. "O Death, Where Is Thy Sting?: Reverend Francis J. Grimké's Eulogy for Harriet A. Jacobs. (With Text)." *The Journal of Negro History* 70 (Winter/Spring 1985): 35–39.

*Sterling, Dorothy. *We Are Your Sisters: Black Women in the Nineteenth Century*. New York: W. W. Norton & Company, 1984.

Stevenson, George. "The Search for the Edenton Years of Harriet Ann Jacobs." *Carolina Comments* 38 (March, 1990): 51–57.

Taves, Ann. "Spiritual Purity and Sexual Shame: Religious Themes in the Writings of Harriet Jacobs." *Church History* 56 (March 1987): 59–72.

Washington, Mary Helen. Introduction/Introduction to Part 1, *Invented Lives: Narratives of Black Women, 1860–1960*. Garden City, N.Y.: Doubleday, 1987.

*White, Deborah Gray. *Ar'n't I a Woman?* New York: W. W. Norton & Company, 1985.

Yellin, Jean Fagan. "*Legacy* Profile: Harriet Ann Jacobs (c. 1813–1897)." *Legacy: A Journal of Nineteenth-Century American Women Writers* 5 (Fall 1988): 55–61.

———. "Written by Herself: Harriet Jacobs' Slave Narrative." *American Literature* 53 (1981): 479–486.